Better

Never 2

NEESH SANTIAGO

Better Late Than Never 2
Copyright © 2023 Neesh Santiago

Books may be purchased in quantity and for special sales by contacting the publisher, Neesh Santiago, at neeshsantiago@gmail.com.

First Edition
Published in the United States of America
by Neesh Santiago

Table of Contents

Better Late Than Never 2

Chapter 1

I stood at the pulpit, sweat dripping down my forehead as the Spirit flowed through me.

"...and the Word of God says that Jesus is the Light!" I thundered.

Amen's could be heard from the people, along with the sound of scattered applause.

"That Light was the light of men, and the darkness could not overtake it. The devil tried to extinguish it, but how many know we serve a matchless Savior!"

A man leapt to his feet in the third row. "Yes, Lord!" he shouted, waving his hands.

The sermon continued as I shared with the people how Jesus came to live with us as a human, how He lived the perfect righteous life, and then how he became the perfect sacrifice so we would have a chance at salvation.

By the time I got to the last of my notes, there wasn't an empty seat in the sanctuary.

My heart filled with joy as I realized that God had done it again. He had delivered a word through me for His people and they had received it, from the looks of things.

My eyes scanned the congregation as I caught one of the ushers discreetly signaling that it was time to close my sermon. My eyes shot to Pastor Blake, who gave me a nod, letting me know that he was the one who told the usher to tell me to wind it up.

I didn't mind because I was finished with my message anyway. Pastor Blake must have had a special announcement he needed to share.

"Well saints," I said, as the music began to play softly behind me. "We spoke a lot today about what Jesus did for us and how he opened the door. In fact, some scriptures even say that He is the Door. But how many know that a door does you no good if you stay outside of it?"

It was remarkable how our musicians were able to easily pick up when a preacher was about to finish his sermon. The music had instantly begun when I lowered my tone, a soft melody playing as a background to my words.

I continued. "What good is a room if there is nobody occupying it? What good is a house if nobody calls it home? The book of Revelation tells us that Jesus stands at the door of our hearts and knocks. He says if any man is willing to open up, He is willing to come in and dine with them. How many want to dine with Jesus today? How many are willing to let Him into their hearts, and accept this marvelous gift of salvation?"

A woman who had her hands raised began rocking back and forth and wailing. The mothers surrounded her, praying.

I looked to the ministry staff who prepared to work the altar today and nodded, then I stepped away from the pulpit, still holding the microphone as I traveled down the two steps that led to the altar. I stood at the center, while the ministry staff stood on either side of me.

"If what I just described sounds like you, and you are willing to let the Lord come in today, come on down to the altar. Don't be afraid."

Before I could finish my sentence, my heart warmed to see several people step outside of their pews from all around the sanctuary. A line began to form, some with tears in their eyes and others holding solemn expressions.

"Praise God, hallelujah," I said, then handed the microphone to a nearby usher. The music that was playing softly increased in volume and the choir began to sing *Fully Committed* by Kingdom. That was one of my favorite gospel songs since childhood. I didn't have much of a voice, but I found myself harmonizing along with the choir as the first person approached me.

It was an older gentleman wearing a tattered suit with tears in his eyes.

I stopped singing to speak with him. "Hey Brother, how are you?"

He swallowed and nodded. "It's my time."

"Your time?" I repeated.

He nodded again. "Yes, I've been running from the Lord for fifty two years. Now it's time to start running with him."

Those words caused a quickening in my spirit. I knew he meant what he said.

"Praise God!" I gestured for him to raise his hands while I grabbed the oil from behind me, gently anointed his forehead, then placed my palm against his forehead and began praying.

"Lord, this brother heard your call. He says he's ready to start his journey with you. Father, we know it is you who draws the hearts of men. We thank you for this dear brother who you have reserved for yourself. Please search him and grant him the ability to repent of his sins, to confess you as his savior, and to allow your Holy Spirit to dwell with his heart. Renew his mind, dear Lord, and give him a hunger and thirst for your Word and your righteousness. All these things we ask in your name, Jesus. Amen."

I hadn't realized my eyes were closed until I opened them and saw the brother on his knees, crying out to God.

"Hallelujah!" he shouted, then he bowed and continued to worship.

I stood silently, worshiping with him for a few moments before he stood and was ready to go to his seat. I knew from scripture and experience that we would never really know the heart of another person, but I would be willing to bet that the brother was truly saved and now embarking on his lifelong journey with the Lord.

I didn't have much time to reflect on that because an older woman was on her way over to me. The line was much shorter than it was when I started praying with the older brother, so there were only a few people left.

I smiled at the older woman, but before she could get to me, a younger woman almost knocked her over, cutting her in line and walking toward me, wearing a skintight dress and a devilish smirk.

I couldn't believe it, but thankfully, before she could get any further, one of the mothers stepped forward and took her hands, steering her away and offering to pray for her.

I was thankful for that, though I was disgusted that she almost knocked over the first woman.

The older woman approached me again and we shared a knowing smile over what just transpired. "Looks like I need to be praying for you, Pastor!" she said, and I chuckled.

"Looks like it indeed. What can I pray for you today, Ma'am?"

A more serious expression crossed her features. "Pastor, I have an appointment this week with the doctor to find out if I need surgery. Please pray for me that I won't need it. I've been following all of his directions, but I feel like..." her voice trailed off as she welled up.

"Say no more, Sister. Let us pray." I anointed her like I did the first brother, then we prayed a heartfelt prayer. After I finished, she prayed for me and that warmed my heart. It wasn't so often that anyone did such a thing.

People thought that because you were a leader, you were perfect and invincible. That couldn't be further from the truth.

Everyone apparently didn't hold that belief, however, because after the service ended, one of the deacons approached me with a stern expression on his face.

"Good afternoon, Pastor Karl."

"Good afternoon, deacon."

He crossed his arms. "Great sermon." He stared as if he was waiting for me to thank him so he could get to the real reason he approached me.

Here we go. "Thank you, Sir. I studied all week for this one."

His lips formed a thin line. "Hm. Studied all week, did you say? Did you happen to run across any scriptures about divorce while you were busy preparing your sermon?"

I should have known.

I had just proposed to my girlfriend of six months, Kenzie, on Friday, but I had been divorced from my ex wife, Marcia, for only a year before we got together. I knew some people would be happy about my engagement, but others would respond exactly like Deacon Brown.

How was I going to get out of this conversation?

I opened my mouth to say something, but one of the ushers approached us. "Pastor Karl, Pastor Blake says he wants to see you in his office."

Thank God almighty, I thought, and couldn't help but to let out a smile as I ended my conversation with Deacon Brown. "See you later, Deacon. You have a good afternoon, now!" I swiftly walked away before he could utter another word.

Thankfully, the conversation with Pastor Blake wasn't anywhere near as disheartening as the one with Deacon Brown. He just wanted to tell me he enjoyed the sermon and ask me to preach again for Youth Sunday, which was in three weeks.

I exited the church in an upbeat mood, but my mind couldn't help but to travel back to the conversation with Deacon Brown.

His response to my engagement was the same as my mother's. My ears were still ringing with what she said to me on Friday after Kenzie's birthday party, which ended up being our engagement party as well.

Mom said she wanted to stay and help me clean up since Kenzie's girlfriends were bringing her home. I should have taken that as a sign of trouble, but I was so high off the fact that Kenzie said yes that I didn't see it.

Once the last guest exited my apartment, she laid into me.

"Karl, we need to talk." Her smile erased immediately.

I was stunned at her sudden change in expression. "What is it, Mom?"

I figured maybe she had another spat with my dad and wanted to vent. My mom and dad had been separated for most of my life, but neither of them had made a move for divorce, even after my father met another woman and had two children by her.

Mom used her hand to lean against the back of one of my chairs, the other hand resting on her hip. "Why didn't you tell me you were planning to propose?"

I got tongue-tied. Mom had dropped hints throughout me and Kenzie's relationship about *moving too fast* and *watching my back*, but the way she just asked that question let me know there was something deeper at work.

"What do you mean, why didn't I tell you?"

She sighed. "Karl, haven't you at least considered talking to Marcia? I know she's been calling you."

My eyes narrowed. "Yes, and I don't appreciate you giving her my number. Marcia and I have nothing to talk about." I got a new phone number shortly after our divorce was finalized.

"Come on, Karl, you were barely married for two years. You can't just throw in the towel that quickly. God hates divorce, and you know it. You need to reconcile with her and stop trying to force a relationship with Kenzie. She's a nice girl, but Marcia is where you belong."

I didn't agree with my mother, but I couldn't deny that her words gave me pause. My marriage with Marcia did end quickly. It was for good reason, since she cheated, but I still felt the shame.

Even though I wasn't the one in the wrong, I couldn't help but to feel like a failure. I was an associate pastor, a leader in the church. People looked up to me for wisdom and advice on how to navigate their lives and marriages, but here I was with a divorce under my belt after two years of marriage, with another marriage on the way.

Had I rushed things by divorcing Marcia?

Should I have forgiven her instead of taking her to the courthouse?

I had told Kenzie I was over my ex, and at the time I believed I was, but now I was wondering if I didn't give myself enough time to heal.

I couldn't just break things off though. What Kenzie and I had was real. But I couldn't block that little voice in the back of my mind that was telling me I made a mistake.

Chapter 2

"Mistake?" My boy Solomon mocked the infamous Soulja Boy tone as he rose from his seat and cocked his head at me. "Did you forget she slept with your day one?"

My mind flashed with anger as I remembered my former friend, Anthony. Visions of him and Marcia in our bed crossed my mind but I pushed them away.

"Preach!" Drew said, leaning back in his seat as he clasped his hands behind his head.

DeMarcus took a more solemn approach. "I don't know, Karl. You did divorce her immediately after you found out."

I couldn't believe my ears. "What would you have done?"

He shook his head. "I honestly don't know, Karl. You know me and Ashley have had our ups and downs."

Solomon's jaw dropped. "What? One of y'all cheated?"

DeMarcus had mentioned him and Ashley having arguments in the past but he never brought up cheating. I assumed their fights were about regular stuff like putting the toilet seat down after using the bathroom and making sure you closed the toothpaste cap.

DeMarcus got tongue-tied. "Wha...who said that?"

"You said *ups and downs*. That's code for, somebody cheated."

DeMarcus fell silent.

I was now intrigued. "Who was it? You or her?"

His ears reddened, which didn't take much since he was light skinned. Then his pupils shifted back and forth. "I made a few mistakes during the first year of our marriage."

"A few mistakes!" Drew said, his chair legs slamming onto the floor as he straightened in his seat. "How many women, bruh?"

"Chill, it was only one woman. Not that that made it right," he stammered.

I studied him. "And she forgave you?"

He swallowed, then nodded. "Yeah, and I will forever be grateful for that. That's one of the reasons I'm saying I can see your mom's side."

I took in DeMarcus' words as my mind went to Marcia. She still hadn't changed her status to single on social media, and I still had her on my friend's list.

As if he was reading my mind, Drew asked a question. "Are you sure you are over her?"

"Huh?" I snapped out of my thoughts.

He shrugged. "I'm saying, you said she's been calling you. Why haven't you blocked her number? And why are you still friends with her on social media? That's low key sending mixed signals."

"What? That's not a mixed signal! Social media means nothing, Drew."

"Yet you blocked and disowned Anthony immediately."

"He was supposed to be my boy!"

"And Marcia was supposed to be your wife."

He had me. Not really, because I was definitely over Marcia, but why hadn't I blocked her? Maybe she was still reaching out to me because she thought there was a chance for us. Especially after... I shook that thought from my mind.

"I'm not trying to make you feel no type of way, Karl," Drew clarified. "I just want to make sure you are making the right decision by marrying a new woman if there is a chance you're not over your ex wife."

Chapter 3

I woke up to a screenshot from my mother of Romans 7:1-3 with the second and third verses highlighted, as if I wouldn't be able to get what she was trying to say.

I couldn't help but to feel bombarded with all the recent happenings since I proposed to Kenzie less than four days ago.

During our relationship, things were smooth sailing, except that one incident where she found out I had been married before.

I was still kicking myself over that, and now I had a new thought. What if I didn't tell Kenzie about my marriage to Marcia because I wasn't over her?

Nah, that wasn't it. I didn't tell her because of the other women I attempted to date, who all had problems with the fact that my divorce was so recent.

I was adamant in my convictions that Marcia's betrayal was enough for me to let go of her completely, but now doubt was creeping in heavily.

I needed to…

My phone buzzed and I stared at the screen, thinking it was my mother again, asking if I got her screenshot.

It wasn't.

A smile broke across my face when I saw it was Kenzie. *Hey boo! Are we still on for tonight?*

I tapped my keypad to respond. *Of course. Where do you wanna go?*

Tonight was going to be our first official date as an engaged couple.

Just that quickly, my worries about Marcia dissipated.

That had to be a good sign, right?

Unless you have feelings for them both, a voice in the back of my mind said.

I ignored it.

***

Kenzie and I greeted each other with a kiss and I pulled back, staring into her soft brown eyes. My woman was fine.

She was filling out that brown bodycon dress and black heels with a black clutch to match. I always loved Kenzie's sense of style, down to the way she wore her hair. Today, she sported curls. I couldn't help but reach out and grab one, pulling it back and watching it spring into place.

Kenzie pursed her lips and cocked her head to the side. "You done?" she asked in a fake sarcastic voice.

I smirked. "One more time," I said, then reached out again, but she swatted me away.

"Boy, stop! You know how long it took to get this style done?"

I held my hands up in surrender. "Excuse me for trying to have fun." I spoke in a playful tone, turning to head to my car.

Kenzie followed and I held the passenger side door open for her so she could get in. Before she could stop me, I grabbed another curl.

"Hey!" she said, slapping my arm as I laughed, then closed the door, walking around to the driver's side.

When I got in, she glared. "Is this how you're going to be when we get married?"

My mouth grew dry, but I refused to let my expression show it. "Every day!" I confirmed in a sunny voice.

She rolled her eyes, but I could tell she liked it.

Kenzie and I had a great time, and the more the night wore on, the less I thought about Marcia.

I dropped her off at home, then headed to my apartment. I couldn't wait til we moved in together. We were waiting until after the wedding, which was in three months.

Only ninety days until...

My dash lit up with a text and I immediately glanced at it, thinking it was Kenzie.

My heart dropped when I saw it was Marcia.

I didn't want to deal with her and I had half a mind to block her like Drew mentioned earlier. I sighed and played the message just to see what she had to say.

Listen, Karl, she had written. *I know you want nothing to do with me, but we need to talk. It's important.*

My nose wrinkled. We needed to talk? About what?

I relaxed as I realized it was probably just a tactic to get me to respond. I never answered any of her calls or texts before.

Maybe this was her final attempt to get my attention before she let me go for good.

I pulled up to my apartment, then reached for my phone to block her.

Before I could get to the text thread, she called me.

I was so caught off by the suddenness of the call that I answered.

"Karl?" she said in a breathless voice.

I didn't respond.

"Karl, please, don't hang up. I need to talk to you."

I stared at the phone. Should I give in? I didn't have anything to say to Marcia since I had no intention of breaking up with Kenzie, but at the same time, I had accidentally answered the phone. It would be rude of me to just hang up.

"What is it, Marcia?" I said with a sigh. "I don't appreciate you calling and texting me. I've moved on, and you should too. I'm engaged now."

She gasped. "What? You're engaged?"

"Don't act like my mom didn't tell you. I know you two are in touch."

"Karl... your mother didn't tell me anything. She gave me your number, but that was it."

That pissed me off. My mom gave her my number, knowing I had changed it because I wanted nothing more to do with her, and didn't bother to tell her about Kenzie? That was disrespectful to the highest degree.

I returned to the conversation. "What is it?"

"Can we meet somewhere?"

"No, we can't. What is it, Marcia?" I didn't mean to be short with her, but she was already working my nerves in a span of less than two minutes.

"There isn't any easy way to say this, but you still need to know."

My ears pricked at those words and I suddenly had a feeling I knew what she was about to say. I prayed that it wasn't what I thought, but...

"I'm pregnant."

Chapter 4

Marcia's words resounded in my ears all night after she spoke them.

This was my worst fear. I almost hung up when she told me she was pregnant, but I knew that I couldn't.

Still, I couldn't help but to try to play her to the left at first. "How do you know it's mine?"

Silence was my reply, then, "Are you serious?" Her tone of voice let me know I was dead wrong for my insinuation. "Come on, Karl, you know I wouldn't even step to you like this if it wasn't."

Bitterness crept into my tone. "I'm just saying. Remember how things ended between us. How's Anthony, by the way?"

"I told you before we got divorced that he was a mistake. I wish you would have listened to me. Karl, I…"

I cut her off. "Listen, Marcia. I've had a long night. I really need to go."

"What do you mean, you need to go? I just told you I was pregnant, Karl!"

Those words stopped me in my tracks. It wasn't that I meant to approach the situation with immaturity, it was that I felt like she was blindsiding me.

"I need time to think. How far along are you?"

"Eight months."

I almost dropped the phone, though I should have known that it had to be at least that long.

"And you waited all this time to tell me?"

"If you remember, I've been trying to..."

"Does my mother know you're pregnant?"

My mind was still calculating now that the news was sinking in. Maybe that was why Mom was so adamant about me and Marcia getting back together.

Marcia cut into my thoughts. "No, she doesn't know. I've kept it under wraps with everyone except my mother and my doctor. Of course, Katrina knows, but that's it."

Katrina was Marcia's best friend.

"Is it a boy or girl?" I asked, though part of me didn't want to know. The more I knew about this baby, the more I would have to accept reality.

I never should have...

"I chose not to have it revealed. I wanted to wait until you knew about it."

I wanted to ask her why she did that, since we weren't together anymore, but I didn't.

What was I going to tell Kenzie?

There was no way this wouldn't cause problems between us. How was I supposed to get married to one woman while I was expecting a baby with another?

You need to call off the wedding.

But I didn't want to.

I found a woman who loved me as much as I loved her.

Marcia never loved me - that was evident in the fact that she was sleeping with my best friend even before we got married.

Wait a minute...

"Are you sure Anthony's not the father?" I asked.

Marcia sighed. "Anthony's dead, Karl."

My eyes bugged out of their sockets. "What? When? What happened to him?"

Although I swore I never wanted to see him again, I didn't want the man dead. We had been friends since childhood. How had I not known?

Then I remembered. I had blocked Anthony from everything.

"He died in a car accident after he moved out of town."

I wasn't aware that Anthony had moved either, but I guessed it was too late to speculate now. After getting off the phone with Marcia, the same question came back to me: What was I going to tell Kenzie?

Chapter 5

I found myself looking back at the scriptures my mom sent me before Marcia told me the news. I knew it was a rabbit hole and would do me no good as far as my current situation, but I couldn't help but to feel convicted.

Granted, what happened between me and Marcia happened before I met Kenzie, but I knew Kenzie wouldn't see it that way.

I could already hear her response. Are you serious, Karl? I thought you told me you were over her!

I was, I swore it.

What happened between me and Marcia was complicated.

It was a weak moment at best.

We slept together twice about a month before Kenzie and I matched on the app. I had just been ghosted by the third woman I was genuinely interested in after I told her about my divorce.

I saw Marcia out at the grocery store. We got to talking and one thing led to another. She seemed lonely, and I had that itch brothers get when we hadn't had any in a while. It was wrong and I knew it, but I fell.

We had sex that night and again the next morning.

Marcia asked me then if I would consider getting back with her, but I was so disgusted with myself I didn't answer.

Look at me now.

I thought I would never hear from her again, until she started calling me over the past couple of weeks.

Why did she wait all this time?

At first I figured she just got the itch again, like I had all those months ago, but at a base level, I had to admit I suspected there was more to it.

We hadn't used protection, so it didn't take a rocket scientist to... Still, I held out hope because it had been so long.

Now I was about to lose the love of my life.

Just as I had that thought, Marcia texted me, then Kenzie.

Marcia was asking to meet up so she could show me the ultrasound photo she had taken months prior, and Kenzie was asking about my day.

I ignored Marcia's text, though I knew I was being childish and answered Kenzie's first.

It was okay. How was yours?

Great. I talked to my girls about the wedding. They are going to help us plan it so we don't need to hire a coordinator.

It was crazy how I was over the moon about me and Kenzie's wedding just a day or two ago, and now my hopes were deflated.

No way was she going to stay with me once she found out about Marcia.

My eyes blurred. Should I tell her now, or wait til we saw each other?

Definitely an in-person type of conversation. One I was dreading, but knew I had to go through with it.

Marcia texted again. *Hello?*

I sucked my teeth. She was already annoying me.

She wasn't annoying when you…

I drew a breath, then responded. *Yes, we can meet.* I contemplated where. My first thought was my mother's house, but I didn't want anyone to know I had gotten Marcia pregnant.

Mom was already on my back heavy about my divorce and engagement. I wasn't subjecting myself to even more pressure any time soon.

Granted, there was only a month before the baby would be here, per Marcia, but still.

Are you sure nobody else could be the father?

I stared at the screen, my hopes rekindled.

No Karl. Like I said before, I wouldn't have stepped to you if I wasn't sure.

24

I swore under my breath, then gave Marcia the address to a nearby park. It was risky, since someone could see us together and raise suspicion, but if I was already in trouble, I might as well deal with it.

Chapter 6

I flipped the ultrasound photo onto Drew's kitchen table, then scraped back my chair and rested my eyes in my palms, elbows on the table before me.

Solomon bugged out. "Whaaa…? I thought you and Kenzie were waiting?"

"Not Kenzie," I mumbled.

After my conversation with Marcia at the park, I couldn't take it anymore. The revelation of her pregnancy was like a ticking time bomb in my head. I went to that park praying that the date on the ultrasound photo wouldn't add up.

Unfortunately, it did.

Marcia let me keep it since she had others from previous ultrasounds.

I studied her baby bump, wondering how I was going to take care of the life growing inside her belly. Not that I couldn't afford it, but how was I going to prepare myself for something like this on such short notice?

I didn't know how I would get over losing Kenzie, but to add a child on top of that?

I contemplated whether this was a cruel prank and whether Marcia was wearing a beach ball under her dress, then as if on cue, the baby kicked and I saw it.

My stomach grew queasy.

Marcia lit up. "Do you want to feel it?" she asked.

I stared at her until her smile turned to a frown.

"Come on, Karl," she said. "I know this might feel like it came out of nowhere, but... maybe it's meant to be?"

I chose not to respond to that question.

"Look, I still need more time to process this. Do you have any more appointments coming up?"

She swallowed, obviously understanding that I was ignoring the elephant in the room but answered me anyway.

"Yes, they will be more frequent now that I'm so close. The next one is Wednesday."

Two days until I had to see her again.

The reality was slamming me like a pile of bricks.

Drew had texted me on my way home and said he and the fellas were playing video games. I said I was on my way without hesitation.

Here we were.

"Karl?" Drew waved his hand over my face.

I blinked and stared at him.

DeMarcus was staring at me. "You said it wasn't Kenzie..."

"Marcia?" Drew offered.

I nodded, then bowed my head in shame.

Solomon let out a breath. "Damn, man. How did this happen?"

For some reason, I tensed and grew defensive. "It was before I met Kenzie. I didn't cheat on her."

Drew's brows furrowed in confusion. "How far along is Marcia?"

"Eight months. She just told me the other day."

"That's foul, bruh!" Solomon said, looking like he was heated for me. "You sure it's yours? You know she was out there."

I perked up. "Out there how?"

If Solomon had information, I was all ears. If there was any inkling this baby wasn't mine, I was running after the possibility full force.

A dark thought crossed my mind that maybe I wouldn't even have to tell Kenzie what happened if it wasn't mine, but I didn't want to go into our marriage with dirty hands. I had already done that before we got together, and it almost cost me our relationship.

"What's good, Solomon?" I repeated. "Marcia was out there how?"

He held his hands up. "Chill, not like that. I meant with Anthony. My bad, I didn't mean to make you think no type of way."

My shoulders slumped. Hope deflated yet again.

"You gotta tell Kenzie," DeMarcus said, as if that wasn't obvious.

Chapter 7

Instead of going straight to Kenzie's apartment like I said I would, I went to my mom's house.

The closer I got to her neighborhood, the sorrier I felt as a man.

Here I was, allowing Kenzie to start planning our wedding with her friends, while I was telling everybody but her that I had a baby on the way with my ex wife.

The news was going to break her heart, I knew it.

I was devastated, though part of me was trying to see the bright side. Children were a blessing, after all. Plus, outside of what Marcia did with Anthony, she was a good wife.

The problem was, I wasn't in love with Marcia, even when we were married. That situation was complicated too, but no time to dwell on it now.

I needed to tell my mom what was going on.

Though she had her ways, my mom was the closest person to me on Earth. She raised me practically by herself after my father left us and started another family of his own.

I didn't have much of a relationship with my brothers and sisters out of loyalty for my mom, and Dad and I barely talked. We were cordial, but he didn't know much about me and I didn't know much about him.

"Hey baby," Mom said when she answered the door. Her eyes studied mine. "You look like something's on your mind. Come on in."

She closed the door behind me and I automatically traveled toward the kitchen. It was second nature for me whenever I visited my mom because she always had something good on the stove. From the mouthwatering smell of things, I was right.

Mom chuckled as I led the way, then she pretended to be upset as I peeked into the pots.

"Boy, I didn't tell you that you could have any!"

I turned to look at her and she had her arms crossed over her chest, but her expression was a proud smile like she knew she had just thrown down on this meal.

"Can I have some?" I asked, sounding like a little boy.

"Let me fix your plate. I don't want you digging through my pots. And wash your hands!" She shooed me out of her kitchen and grabbed a plate from the cabinet.

I went to her half bath to wash my hands as she instructed. Aside from good cooking, Mom's bathrooms always smelled great too. She had a fresh bowl of potpourri sitting on the back of the toilet along with some air freshener.

After I washed my hands, my eyes fell on the hand towels she had hanging on the rack, then I drew back as if I had been shocked. I could hear her now.

Karl, I know you didn't touch my good towels! Those are for decoration!

I shook my head then grabbed a paper towel from the holder that was affixed to the wall. I wasn't sure why I hadn't noticed it before, then I realized it was new. The paper towels used to be behind the toilet where the potpourri bowl was.

"Oh well." I exited the bathroom, returning to the kitchen to see that Mom had already fixed plates for both of us. She was waiting for me to come back before she started her meal, from the looks of it.

"Thanks," I said, then Mom nodded at me and I said a quick prayer.

A few minutes into our meal, she spoke up.

"So what brings you out here to visit me, son?"

I froze, not wanting to talk about it, but I knew I had to. Suddenly, I was no longer hungry. I pushed my plate forward.

Mom's eyes flashed with surprise. "What's wrong, baby?"

Might as well get it out now. "I may have a baby on the way."

She choked on her baked chicken. "What?" Mom grabbed her glass of strawberry lemonade and sucked some down her straw before speaking again. "Karl, are you serious? I wasn't aware you and Kenzie were having sex!"

I swallowed. "It's not Kenzie."

Now she looked puzzled. "Who is it, then?"

I didn't respond.

"Answer me, Karl."

"Marcia," I mumbled, but she still heard it.

Another gasp escaped her lips, and then, "I knew it!"

I looked back up at her. "Huh?"

"I knew it," she repeated. "I kept telling you that you weren't over that girl but you wouldn't listen to me. Now look what happened."

"Mom," I started, but she wasn't finished.

"So what are you going to tell Kenzie? I'm sure she would understand. You and Marcia stood before the Lord. God said that what He put together, let no man tear it asunder."

I didn't know which comment to address first. "Mom, I'm not getting back with Marcia."

She stared at me. "You're not? I thought you said she was pregnant?"

"She is, but it's complicated."

"Complicated how?"

I really should have had this conversation with Kenzie first. I was already exhausted after explaining the story twice. It was nobody's fault but mine, but still.

"It was a mistake," I let out. "Months ago, before I met Kenzie."

Mom wasn't convinced. "Well, it had to be right before you met her, Karl. You and Kenzie have been dating what, four months?"

"We're engaged, Mom, and we dated six months."

Not that it mattered much since Marcia was pregnant, but I was tired of my mother disrespecting our relationship. It was as if she didn't believe what Kenzie and I had was real. My confession had only fueled her fire, I knew it, but it wasn't like I could keep it a secret if she was going to be a grandmother.

Mom softened her tone. "So what are you going to do?"

I shrugged with a sigh. "I don't know, Mom. I have to tell Kenzie but I don't want things to end between us."

We sat in silence for a few months, then Mom said, "Karl, I know this isn't what you want to hear right now, but that might be what's best. You don't want baby momma drama during your first year of marriage anyway. Take this as a sign. Sometimes when we make mistakes, the Lord sends someone or something our way to get us back on track. I know you didn't ask for my advice, but I think you should reconcile with Marcia."

Chapter 8

Kenzie and I usually saw each other at least once a week outside of texts, calls, and FaceTime, but I had sort of been avoiding her. She hadn't noticed yet because she was busy with her girls calling venues and planning our wedding, but I knew sooner or later, I would have to come clean.

It had been six days since I found out the news about Marcia and I had been missing Kenzie like crazy.

Avoiding her made zero sense, but I guessed a part of me was thinking that my avoidance might lead to a miracle. Maybe I would wake up tomorrow and realize this was a bad dream and that I never even slept with Marcia, much less got her pregnant.

Why did this have to happen after I got engaged?

Why wait until she was eight months pregnant to reach out to me?

The more I thought about it, the more infuriated I became. Marcia knew my address just like I knew hers. Why hadn't she stopped by or inboxed me via social media as soon as she found out?

She claimed she had been trying to reach me, but she just started calling my phone a couple of weeks ago, and that was after she got my number from my mother. Why not just inbox me?

I texted her to find out.

She responded a few moments later. *I wrestled with whether I should tell you, Karl.*

Now I was offended. *What do you mean, you wrestled? Did you think I wouldn't take care of my child?*

My phone lit up with a call from her, but I rejected it. Somehow I felt safer that way.

Why are you rejecting my call?

Texting is just fine.

Listen, I don't have time for petty games. I'm eight months pregnant with your child. You need to grow up and handle this like a man!

Like you handled our marriage with Anthony?

Another call came through, and I rejected it.

Does this mean you're not coming to the next appointment?

Why would you think that?

Because you keep rejecting my calls!

You're not my woman, Marcia.

I know that, Karl. You've made that very clear. You know what? Forget it. I'll raise my child myself.

Now I felt like a jerk. I called her and she rejected it.

See how that feels? was her immediate text.

I'm sorry.

Whatever.

A call came through from Pastor Blake.

I straightened in my seat as if he could see me.

"Hello?" I answered.

"Hey, Pastor Karl. How are you?"

"Doing good… how are you?"

"I'm fine. I just got off the phone with your mother and she said you wanted me to call you?"

Heat rushed to my ears. What was wrong with Mom?

"Oh, uh, I…" I was flabbergasted. It was one thing to share with your mom and your friends that you had fallen in the way I had, but it was another level to confess to the pastor.

Still, being an Associate Pastor myself, I knew I had to come clean.

"Pastor, I made a mistake."

"A mistake?" he repeated. "What kind of mistake?"

I went into the story, feeling worse with every word I spoke. This was the third conversation I was having about this child that did not involve Kenzie.

She was never going to forgive me.

As if she heard my thoughts, she texted me.

Hey babe… Want to hang out tomorrow? I feel like we haven't seen each other in ages!

"I'm sorry to hear about what you're going through, son," Pastor Blake said. "Have you spoken with Kenzie about it?"

I swallowed. "No... and just to clarify, what happened with Marcia only happened that one day. I haven't been with her since and Kenzie and I haven't been intimate."

Pastor Blake didn't ask me for this information, but I felt like it was my responsibility to provide it since I was a leader in the church.

"I understand. Thank you for sharing that. Karl, you know I can't tell you what to do in this situation but I do feel your anguish even as you tell the story. Let us pray."

I was blown away.

Not by the fact that he prayed for me, but the fact that Pastor Blake didn't respond in the way I thought he would. I was expecting fire and brimstone or pitchforks or something.

Not that he was that type of pastor, but I had committed fornication.

"I trust you'll make the right decision, son."

When we hung up, I forgot I had left both Kenzie and Marcia on *read*.

I answered Kenzie's text. *Sure, babe. Just pick the time and place and I'm there.*

Chapter 9

I took my time getting ready for me and Kenzie's date. She picked Dave & Buster's, the place we went the first time we kissed.

Guilt consumed me. How was I going to face her and act like nothing happened?

"I guess this is it," I said to my reflection, then began to rehearse how I would approach the conversation.

Before I could finish my train of thought, my doorbell rang.

I sucked in a quick breath. Kenzie told me she wanted me to pick her up!

My mind began racing, but I wasn't going to leave her standing at the door. It was time to man up and face the music.

I shuffled to the front door and opened it, forcing a smile to my face as I prepared to lose the love of my life.

It wasn't Kenzie.

"What are you doing here?" I asked, leaning over Marcia's short frame to see if Kenzie happened to be driving down the street. It was paranoia, I knew, because Kenzie was likely waiting at home for me to pick her up like we discussed.

Satisfied that Kenzie wasn't about to pop out of the bushes, I focused back on Marcia.

I couldn't help but to glance at her baby bump too. It seemed to have grown since the last time I saw her, but that was probably my mind playing tricks on me.

"Aren't you going to invite me in?"

"What are you doing here, Marcia?"

"I was tired of playing phone games. Come on, Karl. My feet hurt!"

I didn't want her in my apartment. If Kenzie showed up, or somebody saw us, it would... The rational side of my brain kicked in and I opened the door wider, stepping aside.

Marcia peered around as she walked side by side with me to the living room.

An indescribable feeling swept through me.

This was wrong.

It was supposed to be me and Kenzie sitting on the couch like this, long after our wedding, and it was supposed to be a joyous occasion.

My anger at Marcia resurfaced, but I fought not to show it. I had been putting my foot in my mouth too much lately as it was.

"What did you want to talk about?" I asked.

"Are you headed somewhere?" Marcia asked, studying my attire.

"Yes, I have a date with my fiancée."

She rolled her eyes. "Way to rub it in."

"Just speaking facts."

"It's not what you're saying, it's the way you're saying it. You keep speaking to me like it's my fault I got pregnant. We both laid down and made this baby, Karl."

That sobered me.

I stared at the floor and humbled myself, then responded. "Sorry. What's going on?"

Marcia's expression changed as if she had just thought of something. "Did you tell Kenzie about the baby yet?"

"No, I didn't. I haven't had the chance to."

She stared as if she knew I was lying but didn't press it. "Anyway, I feel like we should have a serious conversation about what we're going to do. You've made it clear that you're not leaving your girlfriend…"

"Fiancée."

"Right. Since you're not leaving her, where does that leave us? Me and the baby?" She rubbed her belly for emphasis.

"I don't know, Marcia. I'm still trying to wrap my mind around this. You've had eight months to think, but I just found out a week ago. You said you weren't going to tell me about the baby at first. What was that about?"

She sighed. "I imagined that you would respond exactly how you've been responding. I didn't want that kind of stress in my life. I already have to deal with losing you. Dealing with your resentment is like salt on the wound."

I opened my mouth to say I didn't resent her but we both would know that was a boldfaced lie. I had no real reason to resent her, since like she said, we both laid down to make the baby, but I hated that this was happening.

"I'm sorry for making you feel that way. I'll do better going forward."

She gave a half smile. "Thank you." Then her eyes glossed over before she blinked back tears. "When is the wedding?"

I swallowed the lump in my throat. There probably wouldn't be a wedding, but I couldn't bring myself to utter those words out loud. "A few months."

Marcia nodded, then stood. "Well Karl, I won't hold you, but I do want us to have open communication for the sake of the child."

I stood with her. "Me too."

We walked to the front door and I watched as Marcia headed toward her car. It was a silver Malibu, the same one she had when we were together. She turned back and looked at me, then shook her head and reached for her driver's side door.

"What is it?"

She looked back again. "Nothing, it's just..."

"It's just what?"

She burst into tears.

Before I knew it, I was rushing over to console her. "Hey, it's okay," I said. "We're going to figure it out."

She wiped her cheek. "I know," she croaked. "But it's so hard. You've moved on and I feel like I'm going to be all by myself."

"You won't be," I reassured her. "I'll be right there, I promise."

After a few more moments, Marcia was calm enough to drive.

When she left, I texted Kenzie asking for a raincheck.

Sorry babe. I have a crazy headache. Can we do tomorrow instead?

Chapter 10

I did not sleep well.

I didn't know if it was because I lied to Kenzie, or if it was because of the stress I was under, but I had a horrible dream.

I was in a house and at first everything was fine, then I walked into the living room and noticed that the bottoms of the walls were cracking and caving in.

I looked around frantically for something to stop the damage and the floor began to crumble beneath me.

A hole grew in the center of the room and a lamp tipped over and fell inside.

I looked down into the hole and saw nothing but dirt underneath.

Part of my mind was telling me I needed to get out of the house, but the other part was telling me I needed to stay and repair the damage. I didn't know which side to listen to.

I had several other variations of this same dream, back to back.

It was clear to me what the meaning was.

I needed to tell Kenzie what was going on.

I was running late for work since I finally got into a deep sleep an hour before I was supposed to wake up and I didn't hear my alarm.

The workday dragged by and I suddenly couldn't wait to get the conversation over with. I contemplated calling Kenzie on the way home but decided to wait til I parked first.

As soon as I pulled into my parking space, I called her. No more playing around.

It rang a few times before she answered. "Hello?"

Her tone was off. She sounded heated.

Was there an argument with her girls?

"Hey..." I said, my confidence waning. "What's going on with you?"

She chuckled as if she couldn't believe what I just asked her. My heart sank.

She knew.

I didn't know how she knew, but she knew.

"What's going on with me?" she repeated. "Let me tell you something, Karl. You are just full of surprises, aren't you?"

I didn't know what to say. "Kenzie, let me..."

"No, you let me tell you what I need to say!" Her voice rose several octaves. "The last time you lied to me, I forgave you. Now you go and do it again?"

"Kenzie, I didn't lie. I..."

"I just got off a messenger call with your ex wife, Karl! Do you know how humiliated I am? I told everybody at my job and all my friends that we were getting married! And the whole time you're still sleeping with your ex!"

"No!" My body grew hot and cold. "Kenzie, wait!"

She hung up.

This was not happening again.

I didn't even know if she was home, but I hightailed it to her apartment anyway, kicking myself for not having this conversation sooner.

I could not believe Marcia did that.

When we talked the other day, everything seemed fine, and now she goes behind my back to Kenzie?

My heart was beating in my ears as I threw my car in park and raced to her front door. Her car was outside, so I knew she was home. I could only hope she would open the door.

I knocked as if my life depended on it. "Kenzie, it's me! Please, we need to talk!"

After five minutes, there was still no answer, but I was nowhere near ready to give up.

I continued knocking.

Kenzie must have gotten sick of me because the door swung open a few moments later.

Her entire face was red like she had been bawling. "What do you want?"

"Baby, please," I pleaded.

"No, Karl. I'm not going to let you trample my heart again."

"I swear. Let me in and I'll tell you the whole story. I don't know what Marcia said to you but it sounds like she wasn't being truthful."

Kenzie sucked her teeth. "She was lying about being eight months pregnant with your child?"

"It's not what you think, I swear."

Kenzie stared at me like she wanted to believe me. I could also see the look of betrayal which I had nobody to blame for but me. I had ample opportunity to tell her about Marcia, but I kept making excuses and now look where we were.

She let me in and closed the door behind me but didn't make a move toward the couch.

I didn't mind. As long as she talked to me, there was still hope.

"Baby, I'm so sorry," I repeated. "I should have told you as soon as I found out but I didn't know how to say it."

Kenzie was staring at me with her arms crossed and a stony expression across her features.

"How long has this been going on?"

"It hasn't. I swear. I slept with her twice in one night before you and I met. That's how she got pregnant."

Her eyes narrowed. "We've been together over six months, Karl."

"I know, but it happened a couple weeks before we started talking on the app. Baby, I swear. And I hadn't heard from her since until she got my number from my mom and started calling me a few weeks ago. I just found out about the baby."

Kenzie's face scrunched in confusion. "Wait, what? Your mom is in on this too?"

I paused. "No...well, she gave Marcia my number, but she didn't know..."

Kenzie cut me off. "Wow, Karl. I knew your mother didn't like me but I thought it was because we got engaged so quickly. I had no idea it was because she wants you to get back with your ex!"

I didn't like the way this conversation was going. "Kenzie, listen to me. What my mother wants is not a factor. I love her and I want her to be happy for me, but the final decision is up to me. I don't want to be with Marcia. I want to be with you."

Kenzie stood silent for a few moments, then, "Her best friend was the one who started the conversation."

That shocked me, but then again, it wasn't something I would put past Katrina. I listened as she continued.

"I had no idea who she was at first, until she said she had a secret for me about my fiancé, Karl. I was about to block her when she sent the ultrasound photo."

My fists clenched at my sides, but I let her keep talking.

"I thought it was somebody playing on my phone, so I set her straight. Then she added Marcia to the conversation and Marcia sent me screenshots of you and her arguing about the baby."

My neck grew tight, but I held it in.

"We were supposed to get married, Karl," Kenzie finished, her eyes filling up again.

I reached out to grab her arms. "Baby, we can still get married. We can figure it out."

"How, when you have a whole family now with somebody else?"

I couldn't take the pain in her tone.

"Baby please..." I drew in a shaky breath. This couldn't be it. Not with Kenzie. "Kenzie, please." A tear rolled down my cheek.

Her tears were streaming now too. "What other choice do we have, Karl? Nobody is going to believe you coincidentally got her pregnant and had a baby right with her right before our wedding. I hear what you're saying and I want to believe you, but this isn't the first time you lied."

"I didn't lie though! I swear, I just found out last week!"

She shook her head. "Even if you did, that doesn't matter, Karl. I would look like a complete fool marrying you now. Not to mention how we would look to our church families. You're supposed to be a pastor."

Those words burned my ears.

Kenzie wasn't speaking judgmentally; she was stating facts. I already had Deacon Brown breathing down my back about being engaged so quickly after Kenzie and I started dating. I would be an idiot to think he wasn't the only one.

Still, I wasn't ready to give up the fight. I loved Kenzie, and I knew she loved me.

We could get through this.

"Please don't make a decision right now," I said. "Just think about it. I don't want to lose you. I'll do whatever it takes to make this right."

Kenzie stared at me for a long time before she said, "Karl, I think you should go."

Chapter 11

I stumbled up to Drew's door feeling like I just got jumped by a pack of ninjas. Solomon's car was outside, and DeMarcus pulled up behind my car.

It was amazing that their wives all let them spend so much time in Drew's basement. I wondered for a fleeting moment if Kenzie would do the same for me, but then I remembered that there was no more me and Kenzie.

She hadn't officially broken up with me when she kicked me out of her apartment but I knew it was only a matter of time.

I should have told her as soon as I found out.

But would it have mattered?

Maybe my avoidant behavior only proved the inevitable.

For whatever reason, my mind went to the message I was supposed to be preaching for Youth Sunday in two weeks. I usually would have already had a sermon topic by now, but with everything that had been going on, I was drawing blanks.

"Hey," Drew said, then opened the door.

DeMarcus walked in after me and we all dapped each other up before heading downstairs to join Solomon.

"What's up fellas?" Solomon said, the smile dying on his lips when he saw the look on my face. "What's good, Karl?" He asked with a head gesture.

I didn't know any other way to say it. "It's over." I explained how Marcia came to my house to talk about the baby, then went behind my back with her best friend to mess up my engagement with Kenzie.

"That's foul, man!" Solomon said. "That's why I can't stand some of these women. Always causing drama."

Drew nodded, but DeMarcus looked like he had a different perspective.

"Karl, have you ever stopped to consider the possibility that this is of God?"

We stared at him as he continued.

"Like we talked about before, if you slept with Marcia almost a year after y'all divorced, maybe you weren't over her. And then the timing of all this, right after you got engaged to Kenzie... it's kind of telling."

"Yeah, but you're forgetting about the fact that I'm not in love with Marcia. I'm in love with Kenzie."

"You have to feel something for her. You did marry the woman."

I shook my head, ready to share my truth. "No, I don't, and I really wish people would stop saying that. I married Marcia because it was the right thing to do."

Stunned silence filled the room as I continued.

"Me and Marcia started having sex before we got married. She ended up pregnant and my mom and her mom pressured us to tie the knot so our baby wouldn't be born out of wedlock. At that time, I had also just recently accepted my role as associate pastor, so I didn't want to look bad."

I knew everything I was saying was coming as a surprise, but I had to get it out.

"Marcia miscarried a month after our wedding. I felt like an idiot because I only married her to look good in the eyes of people, but at the same time, I figured if we were already in it, we might as well make the best of it. I can't front that I developed a love for her, but I was never in love with her."

"So why sleep with her again after your divorce?" DeMarcus said.

I let out a frustrated breath. "I was being an idiot again. I just got ghosted by the third woman who found out about my recent divorce. Nobody believed I was sincerely ready to be with another woman that soon. I ran into Marcia at the wrong moment."

Solomon spoke up next. "Are you sure you're not rushing things with Kenzie then? If you're saying you only married Marcia out of pressure from other people, is there a chance you're doing the same with Kenzie? Trying to remove the proverbial scarlet letter of divorce?"

"Yeah, but that wouldn't solve his problem anyway," DeMarcus said. "The Bible says pastors are supposed to be husbands of one wife. Karl, I think you might be dodging a bullet here. If you ever want to move up into a senior pastor role, you might be hurting your chances."

That threw me for a loop. "Huh?"

Drew stepped up. "I don't think that's what that scripture means, DeMarcus."

"It is, I've studied it."

I wasn't convinced that DeMarcus was right either, but I wasn't thinking about my role as a pastor in that moment. Not that I shouldn't have been because I did take the office and calling very seriously, but I was more focused on not losing the woman I loved.

My boys had good intentions, but in so many words, they all seemed to believe I should let Kenzie go and get back with Marcia.

In my heart of hearts though, I didn't think that was the right decision.

Chapter 12

Although I had been divorced, I never went and did a deep study on the implications of ending a marriage and what the scriptures said about marrying someone new.

I had taken the day off work since I had to go to an appointment with Marcia and also, I needed a mental break from the responsibilities of my job. I was a corrections officer at a youth detention facility. I loved my guys but helping them through their issues while I was dealing with something so major was taxing.

I whipped up a quick cup of coffee and broke out my Bible and laptop, searching the *Logos* software and multiple websites for scriptures on divorce.

A lot of the information I found was pertaining to the Old Testament, so I skipped most of that. Believers in Christ were under the New Covenant, so our primary teachings would be in the New Testament.

The first scripture I studied was the one my mom sent me in Romans 7, talking about a person being bound to their spouse for as long as they lived.

Almost immediately, I saw my mother's error. She wasn't understanding the context. That set of scriptures was talking about the Law versus Grace. Old Testament believers were bound by or married to the Law of Moses, but with Jesus' death, burial, and resurrection, New Testament believers are dead to the Law. We are under the laws of Christ.

That information made me relax slightly, but I needed to tackle the scripture DeMarcus mentioned next. On my way there, I stumbled across 1 Corinthians 7. As soon as I started scanning that chapter, I felt like I was in trouble, especially when I got to the end. There were some scriptures in there that seemed to say that you couldn't, or at least, shouldn't, get divorced. Other scriptures toward the end seemed to insinuate that a person was bound to their spouse until they died, just like Romans 7.

I would have to study this further to get a better understanding. One day wasn't going to do it.

This was fine with me because I loved studying the Bible, even when I came across something that would give me pause or make me change something about myself.

That was part of being a believer, allowing God to transform you by renewing your mind through His Word.

At the same time, I would be a boldfaced liar if I said I wouldn't care if the scriptures basically said I couldn't marry Kenzie.

I had never been the overtly rebellious type, which in some cases was a problem, because I let other people's perceptions force me into a marriage I didn't truly want.

But now that I was trying to enter a marriage I did want, God might be the one saying I couldn't do it.

It was a lot to think about, but I was determined to get to the truth.

One thing was for certain... no matter what anybody said, I wasn't getting back with Marcia. I didn't love her. I would help her raise my child and love him or her to the best of my ability, but me and Marcia would be coparents.

My mind became consumed with the possibility of having to live the rest of my life as a single man if the scriptures were saying I couldn't be remarried after a divorce.

My phone alarm went off, shaking me from my thoughts.

Time to hop in the shower to get ready for the appointment with Marcia.

Hopefully everything was straight with the baby.

Chapter 13

I pulled up to the clinic and found a space two cars over from Marcia's car. I wondered when she arrived, because I was five minutes early.

I exited my vehicle and walked toward her car. She was gesturing like she was on the phone with somebody, then I heard a voice coming through her Bluetooth.

"Let me know what happens, girl," Katrina was saying.

I fought the urge to suck my teeth, rapping my knuckles on the trunk of Marcia's car to get her attention.

She whipped her head around and I waved.

Marcia ended the call with Katrina, then opened her driver's side door, pausing and taking a deep breath after slowly easing her legs out first. Her ankles were swollen.

It was at that moment that I appreciated the beauty of what women endured when they brought lives into this world.

Even if Marcia and I weren't a couple, she was still carrying my seed. From the looks of things, she was taking good care of herself, keeping up her appointments and eating a healthy diet. Although it was a sight to see, half of my perception was tainted.

This should have been me and Kenzie.

If things didn't work out between us, I would never forgive myself.

Kenzie would move on with another man, most likely. One who never lied or held secrets from her.

And what would I be left with?

A child and an empty space next to me in bed.

I forced those thoughts away and mustered a smile for the sake of peace. "Hey," I greeted her as she waddled toward me.

"Hey."

We awkwardly headed toward the clinic doors and I held the door open for her as she walked inside.

The receptionist's eyes widened when she saw us. "Oh, you're both here today!"

I opened my mouth to ask her what she meant by that when Marcia answered. "Yup, we sure are!"

The receptionist checked us in and we took seats in the waiting area.

Thankfully, the doctor didn't take long to see us, and the appointment was even shorter than the wait time. Marcia was due in less than three weeks.

I needed to mentally prepare myself for the day she gave birth. It was a given that I should be there in the delivery room, but was I ready to hold her hand while she pushed out a child, knowing we wouldn't be sharing a life together afterward?

That's the bed you made, my mind said.

Marcia and I chatted for a brief moment as we exited the clinic, but I couldn't help but to notice the receptionist staring holes through me as we walked out.

She was looking at me like she had something to say and I almost called her out on it, but decided against it.

That woman didn't know me. She probably thought I was some deadbeat who decided to show up at the end of his woman's pregnancy, but that wasn't what this was.

I pulled up to my apartment and was about to exit my vehicle when a FaceTime came through from Kenzie.

I answered immediately. "Hey."

Her expression was neutral. "Hey. What are you doing?"

I didn't want to answer that question because it was like pouring salt on an open wound, but I was done hiding. "Just came back from a doctor's appointment with Marcia."

Kenzie nodded. "How's the baby?"

"Good so far."

"Are you excited?"

Why was she asking me that? No, I wasn't excited, because there wasn't any part of this situation that wasn't messed up.

I sighed. "To tell you the truth, not really."

Kenzie nodded again. "That's actually why I called."

My mouth grew dry. "What do you mean?"

"Karl... I've been thinking, and I don't know if I want to be a stepmother before I even have a chance to have a child of my own. I mean, it would be one thing if you already had kids and I had a relationship with them, but imagine us trying to build a healthy marriage while you're at Marcia's beck and call every day for your new baby?"

My heart sank. Still, I didn't want to just give up. "Kenzie, I understand that, and I'm not denying that it would be difficult but I don't want to throw away what we have."

"That's another issue though. What do we have if this is the second time we've encountered a serious problem involving your ex wife? You didn't even want to tell me she existed at first. Someone else had to tell me. Then you didn't want to tell me she was pregnant. She told me."

"I..."

She cut me off by holding her hand up. "I hear you, you just found out about the baby. I get it. But you never mentioned sleeping with her right before we met. You have to understand why I don't feel like I could fully trust you."

"Kenzie, I would never cheat on you. I never cheated on Marcia! She was the one who was unfaithful in our marriage."

"But even if you don't cheat, you hold serious secrets, and that's a problem."

She had me there.

"You're right." I sighed in resignation, prepared for the inevitability of her next words.

"I'm still processing everything," she said in a lighter tone, "because I obviously don't want things to end between us either, but Karl, I have to be honest with you. I'm not sure this is something I can do."

Chapter 14

I needed a break from life.

Unfortunately, that wasn't possible. Kenzie and I talked and texted a few more times throughout the week, and she didn't mention anything else about whether she wanted to break things off or go through with our marriage.

I didn't bring it up either since it was her decision to make.

I needed to be a better man. I was faithful and loyal and believed I was trustworthy, but was I really?

Kenzie was right about me holding secrets. I also cared too much about what other people thought of my life.

If whatever I was trying to do wasn't sin, other people's perceptions shouldn't matter.

I learned that lesson the hard way by marrying Marcia, only to experience the heartache of miscarriage and the devastation of being cheated on then filing for divorce.

Wait... maybe *that* was the sign. DeMarcus thought God was at work with the fact that Marcia popped up eight months pregnant after Kenzie and I got engaged, but what if it was the other way around? The same thing could be said about me and Marcia's marriage.

She obviously didn't love me if she was sleeping with me and Anthony at the same time. Now that I thought of it, she hadn't mentioned being in love with me when she asked if we could rekindle our relationship. She was more concerned with the prospect of being a single mother. Which was understandable, because my mother was basically a single mother, raising me after my father left us.

What if Marcia's reappearance in my life was a test or trial? What if it really was that me and Kenzie were supposed to be together and not me and Marcia?

If feelings were the determining factor, that was the clear answer.

Being a believer though, I needed to make sure scripture agreed with my decision. Above all, I wanted to do what was right in God's eyes.

I only hoped that didn't mean I had to give up Kenzie.

Ironically, Pastor Blake's sermon today was about the Church being the bride of Christ. He spoke on us being married or united with Christ as believers, then segued into relationships between husbands and wives and how they should treat one another. Deacon Brown stared at me the whole time Pastor Blake talked about marriage, a dignified smirk on his face, but when the pastor spoke on how believers treated each other in general, he turned back around and faced forward the rest of the sermon.

By the time service ended, I was full of questions and desperate for answers. I approached Pastor Blake's office, hoping that he was alone so we could have a conversation.

I knocked lightly.

"Come in!" he said, and I opened the door.

His face lit up when he saw me. "Hey, Pastor Karl! How are you?"

I exhaled. "Not good, Pastor, to tell you the truth."

His forehead creased with concern. "Really? What's going on?" He signaled for me to close the door and have a seat, then he sat behind his desk.

I obeyed and sat across from him.

"Pastor, have you ever done a study on divorce?"

He looked taken aback by my question. "You're thinking of divorce before you even get married?"

I let out a chuckle. "No, not at all. It's just that some things have been going down." I briefly explained my situation with Kenzie and Marcia.

Pastor listened without interruption. I had already told him some of what was going on previously, so I focused on what I wanted to do versus what it seemed the scriptures were saying in 1 Corinthians 7, not to mention the verse in 1 Timothy that DeMarcus brought up.

"I see," he said when I finished. "Well Karl, like I said before, I can't make a decision for you about what to do when it comes to Kenzie versus Marcia, but I can shed light on the scriptures. 1 Timothy has been interpreted multiple ways by different scholars, but the one that seems to make the most sense is that a man needs to be devoted to his wife in order to qualify for a pastoral role. In other words, infidelity would be a disqualification."

"Okay, I get that," I said, feeling lighter all of a sudden. "But what about 1 Corinthians 7?"

Pastor Blake shifted in his seat. "That chapter is understandably more complex because it is dealing with a range of different situations. Paul is discussing married people, single people, virgins, widows, you name it."

I was all ears.

Pastor Blake continued. "According to my understanding, 1 Corinthians 7 is not necessarily saying a person cannot divorce or remarry. There are different schools of thought on how to interpret it, like 1 Timothy, but the one that seems to make the most sense says that it is essentially encouraging people to stay with their spouses and not take marriage lightly. Aside from that, though, why are you feeling like you can't remarry? Didn't you say the reason you divorced Marcia was because she was unfaithful?"

That question hit me like a ton of bricks, then I felt like a fool.

"Yes, that's why we divorced."

He studied me. "And you never felt any discomfort with your decision to divorce her instead of working it out?"

I shook my head. "Never. If it wasn't for this pregnancy, I wouldn't have any association with Marcia. I would be on my way to marrying Kenzie."

Pastor Blake sat back in his seat. "There you have it then, Karl. I think you have your decision; you just have to move forward with it."

By the time I left Pastor Blake's office, I had a better understanding about my situation from a biblical standpoint. I had no idea why I hadn't thought of the basic scriptures that said I had grounds for divorce because of Marcia's infidelity. Maybe it was the stress of finding out about the pregnancy.

An idea came to mind. Maybe me and Kenzie's relationship could be saved after all! I reached for the Contacts button on my dashboard, but before I could go to her name, an incoming call from my mom flashed across the screen.

"Hello?" I answered.

"Hi Karl, do you have a minute?"

"Yes... why, what's up?"

"I need you to stop by my house."

Chapter 15

What could Mom want to talk to me about?

I hadn't been by her house in a while, so maybe that was what it was about. I hoped she didn't call me over to try to convince me to get back with Marcia again.

I headed to her house and she was already waiting in the doorway when I pulled up.

Her expression was unreadable. "Hey," she said. "Come on in."

I entered the house and just like last time I was here, it was smelling good. My mouth watered at the sights of macaroni and cheese, collard greens, candied yams, and fried chicken. Mom already had my plate sitting on the table.

After I said Grace, we dug into our meals. I was starving, so I wolfed mine down.

Mom's bites were much smaller, like she was picking at her food rather than enjoying it. Something was on her mind.

Just like Mom knew me, I knew Mom. "What is it?" I asked, feeling guilty that I hadn't considered she might be going through something as I devoured my plate.

She swallowed, then pushed her plate away. "I owe you an apology, son."

My jaw dropped. "An apology?"

She nodded.

"For what?"

Her eyes watered and she dabbed them with a napkin. "For trying to push my problems onto you."

I wasn't following. "What problems?"

She shook her head. "I wasn't fair to you and Kenzie. I acted very standoffish toward her when she did nothing to me to deserve that. And it was all because I never got over your father."

I was floored, listening on as she continued.

"Karl, the reason your father and I are still married isn't because of him. It's because of me. He's asked for a divorce several times, but I keep putting it off." A faraway look crossed her eyes. "I guess in the back of my mind I was holding out hope that we would one day get back together."

I opened my mouth to say, *but he has a whole other family now,* but closed it.

Mom continued, her lower lip trembling. "I guess I felt ashamed. Even though he cheated on me, I felt like maybe I had done something wrong to deserve it. Maybe I didn't give him enough attention. Maybe I wasn't diligent enough in my wifely duties. And then the sisters at my church didn't make it much better." She became more emotional, and I raced to her side to comfort her. "They treated me like it was my fault he cheated. I heard whispers behind my back about how my husband left me because I didn't know how to please or keep a man. I guess holding onto our marriage was my way of trying to get back at them. If your father and I got back together, I would prove them wrong."

Mom said a mouthful, but I understood where she was coming from. Society as a whole tended to come down hard on women who weren't married. If you were anything but a wife and mother, something was wrong with you. I got it. Kenzie had shared with me previously about how she had dealt with similar feelings with all her friends being married and working on children while she was still single.

I was horrified at the thought that I would only make her situation worse if we didn't work out. Not that marriage was the end-all-be-all but knowing that and living it were two different things.

"Mom, there's no reason to feel ashamed. Dad did what he did, but you got through it. We survived."

She looked up at me. I sensed that she needed more encouragement so I continued.

"Of course, every boy wants his father growing up and I can't front like I don't feel any type of way toward him for what he did, but I watched you push yourself to be the best mother you could be. Any man worth a grain of salt would bend over backward to be your husband."

She burst into a fresh round of tears after that.

I blinked back my own emotions and gave her a deep hug.

Mom and I chatted for another hour or so before I was ready to go home, but first, I needed to stop by Kenzie's.

Chapter 16

Thankfully, Kenzie was home.

The question was, would she answer the door?

I raised my hand to knock but I heard the lock turning from the inside. Kenzie opened the door, then jumped when she saw me. "Karl! What are you doing here?"

She was so beautiful. I took in her angelic features, hopefully not for the last time, before I answered. "I needed to see you. I think I have a solution for us."

Her nose crinkled. "A solution?"

I nodded. "Yes. For our marriage."

Kenzie let go of the door knob, then brushed a curly strand of hair behind her ear. "Karl…"

I sensed she was about to brush me off, so I cut in. "Wait, just hear me out."

Kenzie stared for a second, then let out a breath. "What is it?"

"Why don't we push back the wedding a few months? Marcia is due in two weeks. After she has the baby, I can help her out with the feeding and changing and doctor's appointments, and you and I can still plan our wedding, just for a later date. Maybe six months?"

She lit up for a second before her features darkened again. "Karl, no."

A pang pierced my heart. "No?"

She shook her head. "Even if we push the date back to when the baby is six months, he or she is not going to magically no longer need your help. Your child will still be an infant, and judging from the type of man you are, I know you will want to be hands on. I can't take that from you." Her lip quivered and she looked away.

Her words shocked me. Kenzie thought she was taking something from me? That couldn't be further from the truth.

"Baby, listen." I gently grabbed her chin, turning it so she faced me. "You wouldn't be taking anything from me. Of course, I'll love my child and plan to do best by him or her, but you are my wife. Or at least I want you to be. I don't want Marcia. I want you."

"How can I be sure of that though? It seems like every time I turn around, there's a problem involving Marcia. I don't mean to be judgmental, but I think you pursued me too soon."

My heart thumped in my chest. Not Kenzie too. Everyone had been telling me this, but to hear it from her did something to me.

76

"Kenzie, that's not true. Yes, my divorce was only a year from the time I met you and I did mess up and sleep with her a month before we connected, but it wasn't because I wasn't over her or wanted to get back with her. It boiled down to me thinking with the wrong head."

Kenzie stared at me as I told her the harsh reality of me and Marcia's marriage, about how we had been pushed together by our mothers because she got pregnant and nobody wanted us to have a child out of wedlock.

"Wait, are you telling me you already have a child?" Alarm filled her features.

"No!" I quickly dismantled that fear. "She miscarried right after we got married." I went on to recap what happened with Anthony. "So you see, it was never about love between us. I was more focused on pleasing other people. But that's not what it is between me and you. I love you, Kenzie, and I know you love me too. What we have is nothing like me and Marcia."

I could tell by the slight change in her expression that she wanted to believe me, but still held reservations. That was nobody's fault but my own.

I opened my mouth to say something else, but she beat me to it.

"I gotta go. I'm running late for Zena's baby shower."

I had totally forgotten about the event. Kenzie's friend Zena had gotten pregnant around the time Kenzie and I started dating and her baby was due in a couple of months. Kenzie and I were supposed to attend the shower together but for obvious reasons, that was no longer happening.

I watched as she locked her door, then started toward her car.

"Wait," I said, desperate to hear what she was thinking.

She turned back.

"Did you forget the gift?"

Her eyes opened wider and she rushed back into her apartment without answering, coming back outside with a huge *Blue's Clues* bag. For some reason, that did something to me.

I studied Kenzie and saw the pain in her eyes. It mirrored my own.

"Hey." I gently grabbed her arm. "Are you okay?"

She nodded, though I knew it wasn't true. "I will be."

"Do you need help carrying that?"

"No, I got it."

Kenzie popped her trunk and put the bag in, then slammed it shut and walked around to her driver's seat. She looked at me before getting in. "I'll think about it, Karl."

I had no choice but to accept that answer.

Chapter 17

I called and texted Kenzie a few times since Zena's baby shower, but she didn't answer my calls and her texts were one-or-two-word answers.

It was time to face reality.

She was breaking up with me.

I had been fighting so hard to hold out hope, but something inside me told me I was fighting a losing battle. Everything I was facing was a consequence of my own actions. I swore, if by the stroke of a miracle, Kenzie took me back, I was never keeping a secret from her again and I was never going to live my life by other people's opinions.

I understood the scriptures about people-pleasing loud and clear now.

Marcia had another appointment today. She was ready to pop at any moment.

The receptionist from last time was there again, wearing that same expression she wore at our last appointment.

I wanted so bad to say something to her, to tell her I wasn't some deadbeat who showed up at the end of his woman's pregnancy to help with the child, but once I thought about it further, it dawned on me that her opinion didn't matter. She didn't know me or Marcia from a can of paint.

The doctor was all smiles. "Looks like things are moving along nicely!" she said. "How are you feeling, mom?"

Marcia smiled. "I'm feeling good, just ready for the baby to come."

The doctor nodded. "You're almost there!" She looked at me. "Have you two discussed names yet?"

Marcia answered before I could open my mouth. "I was thinking Tina if it was a girl, and Karl Junior if it was a boy."

I was floored. Karl Junior? She wanted to name the baby after me?

Marcia and I needed to have a serious conversation after this. Not that I was opposed to having my child named after me, but it didn't feel right with the situation we were in.

At the same time though, if it was a boy, that would make him my first-born son. I wouldn't want him to think I was rejecting him by not giving him my name because I was reserving it for children I would hopefully have with Kenzie.

My mind went back and forth to the point that I didn't hear another word from the doctor or Marcia's mouths for the rest of the appointment.

When it was over, I walked Marcia to her car, then headed to my own.

I was zoned out in my driver's seat before I noticed that there was a folded white sheet of paper tucked into my windshield wiper.

I cocked my head back. What was that?

Exiting my vehicle, I approached the paper with caution. I had heard stories of people having things left on their windshields or door handles, only for it to be some toxic drug.

The wind blew and the paper flapped open, showing a few words scrawled inside. I craned my neck to see them, then decided to take a chance and grab the paper, opening it to read what was written.

Thankfully I didn't drop dead, so I guessed it wasn't drugs.

But the contents of the message made the hairs on the back of my neck stick up.

Everything is not what it seems. Text this number if you want to know the truth.

What the hell was this? Some kind of elaborate scam designed to get me to go somewhere so I could be jumped or robbed?

I had half a mind to throw the note away, but the other part of me couldn't help but to be curious. Had they left this paper on the right car? What information could they possibly have for me? These scammers were good, I had to give it to them.

I wrestled with it for a few more moments before hopping back in my driver's seat, tossing the note on the passenger's seat. As I pulled out, my eyes shot to the space where Marcia had been parked.

She was long gone.

Chapter 18

I took a chance and texted the number when I got home.

My reasoning was that if it was a scammer, I would know immediately anyway. I wasn't clicking on any links or agreeing to meet at any secret locations.

Hey, I wrote. *I got your note.*

Seconds later, the scammer responded. *Good. I was hoping you did.*

Was this a man or a woman? *Who are you?*

It doesn't matter who I am. It matters that I have information you need to know.

I sucked my teeth, not here for whatever game they were trying to play. *Information about what? I'm not sending you my cash app info.*

Lol... I'm not a scammer.

How would I know that?

Your name is Karl, right?

My eyes bulged. This was someone I knew? Who did I know who would do something like this?

My mind went to Drew, Solomon, and DeMarcus. Though we laughed and joked together all the time, I didn't think any of my boys would send me a random note. Plus, none of them knew I was going to the appointment with Marcia anyway. Unless they were tracking my moves, which would be weird, it wasn't one of them.

Who are you?

Like I said, it doesn't matter who I am. It's what I know that matters.

I don't have time for riddles. What do you know?

It's about your child.

My fingers paused in the middle of the sarcastic reply I was submitting. Were they talking about the baby with Marcia? My mind went back to the waiting room at the clinic. None of the patients struck me as suspicious.

Everybody seemed to be ready to get their appointments over with.

I don't have any children.

I'm talking about the one on the way.

So it *was* somebody from the doctor's office. The receptionist? No, it couldn't have been her. Every time I saw her, she stared at me like I stole something.

Who are you? I asked again.

Meet me at Barber Park on Thursday at four o'clock. I'll be near the benches by the swings.

This whole situation was suspicious as hell. I got a random note on my windshield and now they

85

were telling me to meet them somewhere? Wasn't this what I just told myself I wasn't doing?

Yet here I was, contemplating going and wondering what information they could possibly have about my child with Marcia.

Part of me was saying to leave it alone because it could still be a scam, but the other side sensed that this wasn't a scam, just a person who had a strange way of operating. If whoever this was saw me at the doctor's office, why didn't they just approach me then?

Maybe it's someone who knows me and Marcia, I reasoned.

I needed a second opinion.

My first thought was to call my boys, but my fingers went to Kenzie's name in my contacts.

Chapter 19

Kenzie answered on the third ring. "Hello? Karl, I didn't make my decision yet."

She sounded annoyed to hear from me.

"I know, I didn't call to pressure you. I got a note today."

"A note from where?"

"I had a doctor's appointment with Marcia and somebody left it on my windshield."

"What did it say?"

"They gave me a number to text. I texted it and they said they have information about the baby."

"Information about the baby?" Kenzie spoke in a bewildered tone.

"Yes. I want to see what they have to say but the way this happened has me suspicious. If someone I know has information, why not just tell me directly? Why leave a note on my car and send me on a wild goose chase?"

"I'm not following... so they never told you what information they had?"

"No, they want me to meet them at Barber Park on Thursday." Thursday was in two days.

Kenzie remained silent.

"Do you think I should go?"

"If you want to."

"Do you think it's safe? What if this is a scam and somebody is trying to jump and rob me?"

Kenzie chuckled, and her amusement was music to my ears. "Karl, I doubt that somebody is trying to jump and rob you. Barber Park is full of kids during that time. Maybe the person has a kid that goes to Benson Elementary."

That made sense. Benson Elementary was right next to Barber Park. Maybe the person was just as nervous about meeting me as I was about meeting them. Which made me suspect it was a woman. But if she was so afraid, why not just tell me what she had to say over the phone?

"I'm not sure if I should trust this."

"I think you should go. I'll go with you."

That shocked me. "You will?"

"Yes, Karl. If they have information about the baby, it probably means Marcia is lying or something. I would love to hear that news."

My heart fluttered. I would love to hear that news too. "That has to be it, right? But I'm still not understanding why this person won't just say that."

I texted the number. *Why do we have to meet? Can't you just tell me the information over the phone?*

The person texted back. *It's complicated. It needs to be done in person.*

That only raised my suspicions even more.

I told Kenzie what just transpired.

"I think we should go, Karl. The park will be busy, so it's not like we're going to get jumped in front of a bunch of kindergarteners."

"Alright, bet."

We ended the call, and I had the glorious feeling that me and Kenzie had turned a corner. I loved the way she said *we.*

Chapter 20

I breezed through my workday, excited about the chance to see Kenzie and hopefully learn that Marcia was lying about the baby.

I had asked Marcia several times if there was a chance I wasn't the father, but she was adamant that I was.

Still, if this person had information that would turn the tables, I was all ears.

When I got off work, I headed directly to Kenzie's house. We only had twenty minutes to get to the park.

"Hey," she said when she opened the door.

She reached up to give me a hug and I kissed her without realizing it.

I pulled back quickly, hoping I hadn't ruined the moment.

Kenzie wore a dazed expression but didn't seem angry. I chose not to say anything.

We traveled to my car and I held her door open like I always did before getting in the driver's seat.

"Hopefully good news," I said, glancing at her after pulling onto the street.

She let out a murmur of agreement.

I wondered what she was thinking but didn't want to press her. She was going with me to meet the mystery woman, that was a good sign.

What if it was bad news?

I couldn't see how it would be, but there was always a chance that whatever she had to say would drive a deeper wedge between me and Kenzie. We certainly didn't need that. I had half a mind to call it off and tell Kenzie I was meeting the woman alone, but that would only make her suspicious.

Just take it as it comes, Karl, I told myself.

We pulled up to the park and just as suspected, it was full of kids and parents. Kenzie and I walked up and approached the bench near the swings as instructed. I scanned the crowd and no one looked suspicious or familiar.

I hoped we didn't come all the way out here for no reason.

My phone buzzed in my pocket. I pulled it out to check the message.

You were supposed to come alone.

My head shot up and I looked around, but again, no one seemed out of the ordinary.

"What is it?" Kenzie asked.

I showed her the message and she sucked her teeth. "Give me the phone."

I handed it to her and she typed a message. *What are you afraid of? Show yourself.*

I watched as a new message popped up on the screen.

No. Tell Karl to come back tomorrow, same time, or he can forget it.

"Oh my God," Kenzie said in an irritable tone.

Her reaction mirrored my own.

"What do you think we should do?" I asked.

She rolled her eyes. "Obviously you will have to come back tomorrow. I can't believe this."

The little hope I had built up deflated. It seemed like me and Kenzie were getting on the right track, but now I wasn't so sure. Maybe she only came because she wanted to hear what the lady had to say and not because she was interested in getting back with me.

I tested the waters.

"Well, since this was a waste of time, are you hungry?"

We stared at each other for a few moments before Kenzie said, "No, I already ate."

Chapter 21

I was completely pissed by the time I got home. Kenzie barely said two words to me when I was dropping her off.

Why didn't the lady just come forward? It wasn't like we were going to hurt her!

I called Marcia, ready to get to the bottom of this.

"Hello?" She answered as if she had just woken up.

I got right to it. "What's going on with you?"

"What do you mean, what's going on with me?"

"I'm going to ask you one more time, Marcia: Are you lying to me about this baby?"

"Karl, you have been with me to the appointments. I'm not hiding a soccer ball under my dress."

"I'm not talking about that and you know it."

"Where is this coming from?"

"I think you're lying to me."

"What reason would I have to lie to you?"

"Because that's who you are!" I knew I was treading in dangerous waters, especially if I wanted answers, but what happened today with Kenzie made me furious. "You lied to me when we were married, knowing the whole time you were sleeping with Anthony. Why did you marry me instead of him anyway? Was that baby even mine?"

It was a low blow and I knew it, but at the same time, that question had never crossed my mind. What if me and Marcia's whole marriage was a sham, outside of the fact that we only did it because of the baby? If I would have found out that I was raising another man's child, I didn't know what I would have done.

Marcia spoke her next words in a low tone. "Listen, Karl, I don't know what's gotten into you, but if you don't want to be a father to your child, you could just say that."

"Nobody's..."

CLICK.

Guess I deserved that for coming at her the way I did. I planned to be cordial with my conversation but I let my emotions take control.

Sighing, I went to her name to call her back, but she was already calling me.

"Hello?"

"And let me tell you one more thing! Don't you ever come to me talking crazy like that again. I am not a whore, Karl. Yes, I cheated while we were married, but you weren't perfect either. None of us are. I owned up to my mistakes."

I couldn't believe my ears. "Nobody said I was perfect but you're not about to sit here and act like my imperfections gave you the right to sleep with my boy. Why did you choose me to marry anyway? Why wouldn't you tell him the baby could have been his too? Or did you, and he rejected you?"

Marcia was silent for a second before she responded. "You know what? This is what I'm not going to do. Don't call my phone again. I will let you know when I'm in labor."

CLICK.

I wasn't calling her back. I was wrong for saying things the way I did, but Marcia couldn't deny that my questions were valid.

My phone buzzed with a text and I swiped it open, thinking it was Marcia, cussing me out again.

It was Kenzie. *Are you going to meet that lady tomorrow?*

I sighed, feeling myself calm. *Yes. If she has information that could help, I want to know it.*

Tell me what happens.

What if she tells me Marcia is lying?

Ten minutes passed before Kenzie wrote back. *We will cross that bridge when we get there, Karl.*

Kenzie, I swear, I will never withhold information or lie to you again.

I hoped she saw I was serious. I prayed she would give me another chance.

My phone buzzed again five minutes later and I eagerly checked the message.

But it wasn't Kenzie, it was Marcia.

Listen, I'm sorry about hanging up on you. That was wrong. You have every right to question me, but I've been under a lot of stress with the baby. My back hurts, my feet hurt, and I just want our child to be healthy. I'm sorry.

I sensed sincerity in the way she wrote her message.

I'm sorry too.

Chapter 22

I woke up to another text from Marcia.

I've been thinking... Wouldn't it be easier if we got back together for the sake of our child? I want him or her to grow up in a two-parent home.

I didn't bother to respond because I didn't want things to get out of hand again.

There was no way I was getting back with Marcia. I understood she was in her feelings with the baby coming any day now, but just like I knew we shouldn't have slept together after our divorce, she knew it too.

Are you going to answer me? She texted when I slipped my phone into the holder in my air vent.

I didn't have time for this, but I didn't want to leave her hanging either. *I don't think that's possible. I'm in love with another woman.*

A few seconds, and then, *But how would that work with us though? I don't know your fiancée and I don't feel comfortable with her being around my child.*

This chick had a lot of nerve. She was the baby's mother, I got that, but did she think I would be dumb enough to put my child in harm's way, much less marry a woman who would hurt them?

That's not really your concern. The baby won't be out of my sight.

I have no way of knowing that.

I felt myself heating up, so I chose not to respond to that message. Marcia was not about to be controlling my moves when I spent time with my child. Fathers had rights too.

When I pulled up to my job, Marcia texted me again. *I'm not trying to make you feel any type of way, Karl. It's just that this is my first child and the situation is complicated. I already feel attached.*

I attempted to be cordial. *That's understandable, but you must realize that I'm not going to let anything happen to the baby.*

I got you. I guess we will cross that bridge when we get there.

This was a headache waiting to happen, I could feel it.

Maybe Marcia would calm down once she saw that I wasn't a threat to the baby. If Kenzie took me back, maybe we could arrange for them to meet in person so Marcia could be comfortable.

I entered the facility and focused on work for the rest of the day. I had a meeting with the mystery woman at four, and I could not wait to see what she had to say.

I was supposed to get off at three, but at two-thirty, my supervisor approached me. "Hey," he said.

"What's up?"

"Reg said he's going to be late. Can you stay til five?"

My jaw dropped. This couldn't be happening when I was this close. "I'm not sure if I can do that. I have an appointment at four."

He studied me. "I understand, but it's your turn to be forced. We need the coverage."

The way my job was set up, we had mandatory overtime when someone called out or showed up late. The correctional facility had to have a certain number of officers on shift at all times.

I fought to remain calm. "Okay, I gotchu."

"Thanks." He shot me a thin-lipped smile and walked off.

I took a bathroom break and texted the woman. *Hey, can we meet at five-thirty? My job is making me stay late.*

I paced back and forth as I awaited her response. *Fine. But make sure you're alone.*

Chapter 23

Finally.

My shift was over so I hightailed it to Barber Park.

On the way there, I stopped at my apartment and grabbed my Glock.

As soon as I concealed it in my waistband, a thought struck me. *Is this considered a secret?* I never told Kenzie I owned a gun.

I didn't necessarily feel like I needed it to meet with this woman, but just in case, I was bringing it.

After thinking a few more moments, I reasoned that I should tell Kenzie about the gun. I didn't want her to be scared off if she did take me back. Maybe she had an aversion to firearms.

I pulled up to the park and it wasn't as busy as it was yesterday. It made sense because most parents probably let their kids play there directly after school then brought them home. I sat on top of the bench by the swings, my elbows resting on my knees, hands clasped in front of me as I leaned forward.

I was so deep in thought I hadn't noticed the receptionist from Marcia's doctor's office approach me.

"Hey," she said.

I startled, then stared at her. "So it was you."

She nodded. "Yup, it's me." She sat near me on the bench, but pulled out a magazine as if she was reading it as she spoke.

Why was she acting so strange? Was this a setup? My head whipped around. I half expected a group of men to be storming toward me with baseball bats.

My Glock felt heavy on my waistband. I couldn't wait for this conversation to be over.

"What information do you have?" I asked.

She didn't look up from her magazine. "Like I said, it's about the baby you supposedly have on the way with that Marcia woman."

The way she said that let me know she didn't know Marcia personally, but to my recollection, she didn't know me personally either, so what were we doing here?

"Okay..." I prodded. "Spill it, please."

She sighed, but still didn't put the magazine down. Instead, she turned the page, then checked her phone before responding.

"I have reason to believe the child isn't yours."

"Okay..." I repeated. "And why do you believe this? Do you know Marcia?"

She shook her head. "Not personally, but we are in a social media group together."

The woman went on to explain how her, Marcia, and Marcia's best friend, Katrina, were all part of a single women's group.

"One day, an anonymous post was put up in the group by a woman saying she was seven months pregnant with a baby, but there was a chance that one of two men was the father. The problem was, there was no way she could be with the first man because he was married. The second man was her ex husband, but he was newly engaged."

My ears were on fire hearing this news. If this woman was telling the truth, Marcia was getting cursed clean out.

"Wait..." I said. "How do you know the anonymous poster was Marcia though?"

She finally put the magazine down beside her. "That's where it gets iffy. Naturally, I was curious as to who the woman was because most of the people in the group were local despite it being open to everyone in the country. Me and a girlfriend started looking through everybody's profiles and we narrowed it down to a few women who had posted pictures of their baby bumps. Marcia was one of them, of course. Then we went back and looked at the anonymous post and saw that although most women were calling her a whore, there were a few who defended her.

Marcia's best friend Katrina was the main one defending her, saying she should tell the engaged man that the baby was his since the married man would most likely not leave his wife."

This was crazy. Absolutely crazy.

"I find this hard to believe. Who are you, really? And how could you have possibly connected this to me?"

She was silent for a moment, then said, "Marcia came to our clinic quite a few times during her pregnancy and I noticed there was never a man with her, nor did she have a ring on her finger. Since I suspected it was her, I did some more digging on her page and saw that her status said she was still married. It didn't show who she was married to, which was strange, but I looked through her photos again and found the wedding pictures with you and her in them. I went to your page and saw your status as engaged."

"Okay... But why would you go through all this trouble to track me down and let me know what was going on? It still doesn't make sense."

She tensed. "Listen, you can't tell anyone what I'm telling you. According to my job, I have to follow HIPAA laws. I agreed to meet with you in person so there was no way to prove I was the one who gave you the information."

"Okay, I'm not going to tell on you."

She faced me directly for the first time since our conversation started. "You sure? I'm not trying to get fired or worse, Karl."

"You have my word. I want this situation to be over with. Marcia will never know how I found out."

She seemed satisfied with my response, so she continued. "Once I saw that your status said Engaged, I naturally looked to see who you were engaged to, and it was Kenzie."

"Kenzie?" I repeated. "You know Kenzie?"

She nodded. "Yes, Kenzie used to work at the clinic with me, but there was this big blow up and... let's just say she inadvertently saved me from a beatdown."

My jaw dropped. I remembered Kenzie telling me a story about her old job and how a woman came in, thinking she was sleeping with her husband, who was one of the doctors at the clinic. The true mistress stood there and watched while other coworkers pulled the disgruntled wife away from Kenzie. Kenzie ended up quitting that job and starting her current job.

"Wow..." My mind was spinning as all the pieces of the puzzle connected. "So you're basically not helping me, you're doing this for Kenzie."

She nodded. "I never got over that day and how if that woman would have broken free, Kenzie could have been seriously hurt over something I did. I wanted to repay her."

As convoluted as the story was, I believed the receptionist.

Even though there was a chance I was still the father, there was also at least a fifty percent chance I wasn't.

"Thank you," I said. "You have no idea how much you've helped."

Chapter 24

Once I left the park, I hightailed it to Marcia's house. If she was the anonymous poster in that group, which I believed she was based on everything I heard, she had some explaining to do.

I pulled up and banged on her door like I was the police.

Marcia looked frightened when she answered, but slightly calmed when she saw it was me. "Karl, what are you doing here?"

I fought to rein in my emotions. "Can I come in please?"

She opened the door wider and I entered. I counted down from ten in my head then jumped right into the conversation. "I've been thinking about everything that's happened since you told me about the baby and I want a DNA test."

"A DNA test?" she repeated, then sighed. "Karl, we already went through this."

"Yes, we went through it, but I have reason to believe you're a liar."

Damn it! I hadn't meant for that to slip out. Of course, Marcia became offended.

"Are you serious?" She scrunched her face like she couldn't believe me. "After that whole argument we had the other day where you ended up apologizing, you're still coming back with the same thing?"

"Yes I am."

"Who else do you think the father is, Karl? I already told you Anthony was dead."

At those words, I pulled out my phone. If Marcia was the anonymous poster, was there a chance Anthony wasn't dead, and that he was the married man? I went to my Block list and unblocked his social media page. My heart sank when I saw all the posts of condolences. But that still didn't mean Marcia hadn't slept with another man.

"Did you find what you were looking for?" Marcia said in a sarcastic tone.

"Not really," I countered. "Who else were you sleeping with around the time you slept with me, Marcia?"

"What are you talking about, Karl?"

"Stop the BS. I have it on good faith that you were having sex with at least one other man around the time we slept together."

"Where are you hearing this from? You know what? I'm tired of..." Marcia stopped mid-sentence, then started breathing heavily. In through her nose, out through her mouth.

"What's wrong?" I asked, my anger dissipating. "Is it the baby?"

She continued breathing for a few seconds. "I don't know... I..." She clutched her belly. "I think I'm having contractions."

My mind went into panic mode. I drove to Marcia's house looking for answers, but it looked like I was about to come out with a baby.

"Come on," I said, and brought her to my car.

She had another contraction on the way to the hospital. When we got there, they took her right in and proceeded to examine her.

I couldn't believe this was happening.

A child was about to be born, and there was a chance I was the father.

Until twenty minutes later when the doctor came in and explained to Marcia that *just like they told her over the phone* earlier that day, Braxton Hicks contractions were normal during the third trimester of pregnancy. She wasn't in labor.

Heated wasn't the word.

Marcia faked going into labor because she didn't want to finish a conversation with me.

I was so disgusted I threw forty dollars at her and told her to order an Uber or a cab home.

Instead of going to my house, I went to Kenzie's. We needed to figure out how to get to the bottom of this.

Thankfully, she opened the door for me without incident and I immediately launched into the story of what happened that day, starting with the receptionist and ending with what just happened with Marcia.

"Are you serious?" she said when I told her that the doctor basically exposed her lie.

"Yes, apparently she had called them earlier and told them her symptoms and they told her exactly what it was. Here I was, thinking the baby was coming and rushing her to the hospital, when the whole time she knew nothing was happening. I can't believe I never suspected Marcia was this bad of a liar."

Kenzie shook her head. "My mind is still blown at how Serita was the one who helped expose the fact that she was sleeping with a married man."

At first I was about to ask who Serita was, but I realized that must have been the receptionist's name.

"What do you think I should do?" I asked.

Kenzie shook her head, then her eyes lit up. "Wait... I think I know something that might work."

I listened as she explained a plan to get Marcia to consent to a DNA test. We could obviously petition for one through the courts, but if Marcia drug her feet about it, who knew how long that could take? Kenzie's plan sounded solid, so I was going with it.

"A'ight, bet. I'll let you know what she says."

Kenzie smiled, and I turned to leave, but stopped short.

"Oh, one more thing." I turned around to face her.

"What is it?" she asked, looking puzzled.

"I brought my Glock to the meeting with Serita, just in case."

Kenzie wasn't following, I could tell from her facial expression.

I clarified. "I own a gun. Just wanted to let you know."

"Oh, that?" She waved me off with a chuckle. "Thank you for telling me, Karl, but no worries. I have a pistol of my own."

That threw me for a loop because Kenzie didn't strike me as the gun-carrying type.

"Really?"

She nodded with a smile. "Yup. My girls convinced me to get one when we went to the gun range."

I grinned in surprise. "Okay, let me find out, Miss Kenzie! Don't tell me you're an undercover gangsta."

She smirked. "I can't confirm or deny it, but don't be the one to *mess around and find out*."

My heart was filled with glee as I drove home from Kenzie's house.

For the first time in what felt like ages, we joked together. I prayed that was a sign from God that everything was going to work out.

Later that night, visions of Kenzie posing with her gun in sexy lingerie filled my mind. I was so turned on I had to take a cold shower.

Chapter 25

I put Kenzie's plan into action early the next morning.

Hey, I texted Marcia.

What do you want, Karl? She shot back.

Listen, I'm sorry about what happened yesterday. I was stressed out about some things that have been going on lately, but... can we talk? I need to see you.

Need to see me for what? Every time you come here, you come with accusations.

I played it smooth. *Yes, I understand and I'm so sorry. I promise I'm not coming to start trouble. Are you hungry? I can bring us breakfast.*

A few moments passed, then she responded. *Yes. I'll text you my order.*

Marcia sent me her order for a breakfast spot downtown. I went and got the food, then headed to her house.

When she opened the door, she studied me like she was suspicious before letting me in.

We went to her kitchen, where I made a show of pulling out her chair for her before she sat down.

"Thank you," she said with a surprised smile and a blush.

It turned my stomach, and for a second I felt like scum because this was all an act. Still, sometimes you had to resort to desperate measures to get to the truth.

I faked a blush of my own, then asked if she wanted me to grab her a plate from the cabinet for her food.

"Yes, please," she said with another smile. "And can you grab the orange juice from the fridge?"

"Sure can!" I handed her a plate and some utensils, then poured both of us glasses of orange juice.

Marcia had already spooned out some home fries onto her plate, so I handed her the container filled with bacon.

"Thank you, Karl. I was starving but didn't feel like cooking."

I nodded. "It's the least I can do for how I treated you yesterday."

She proceeded to eat her food.

I said Grace and silently prayed the Lord would forgive me for what I was about to do. Then I started eating my own food.

Halfway through our meal, I approached the subject. "Marcia, I've been thinking."

She paused mid-bite. "About what?"

I swallowed, then put my fork down to give her my full attention. "We've been having a rocky few weeks, but it was mostly my fault. To tell you the truth, all those times I came at you weren't about anything you did. I was upset because Kenzie broke things off with me."

Marcia gasped. "She did?"

I nodded with a pain-filled smile. "Yes. We broke up as soon as you told me about the baby, and I told her, but to be honest, I don't think we would have ended up together anyway."

Marcia was all ears. "Why not?"

"Because Kenzie has a lot of issues. She's immature and judgmental for starters. And also very controlling. Even though she broke up with me, yesterday I realized that it might have been for the best. Rushing you to that hospital because we thought you were in labor did something to me."

Marcia stared. "What are you saying, Karl?"

I went in for the kill. "This is going to sound stupid, but I think you were right all along. If me and you are about to have a child together, it only makes sense for us to try to make it work. I don't want my child to grow up separated from his father."

Marcia's eyes filled with tears. "Are you serious?"

I swallowed again and nodded. "I think it's for the best."

She wiped her mouth with a napkin. "Okay, well I'm willing to try it if you are. Would we get remarried? Or would we take it slow?"

I paused as if I was contemplating it. "I think remarriage makes the most sense, but first, I do want to be absolutely sure he or she is mine."

Marcia looked like she was getting upset, but I held a hand up to stop her.

"No, not like that. It's more for my peace of mind. You may not understand, but as a man, I just need to see the proof with my own eyes."

This was the part of the plan that was kind of sketchy, but I was praying it worked.

To my surprise, Marcia agreed. "I can understand that," she said with a nod. "I believe we can initiate the test when the baby is born."

Chapter 26

Kenzie and I talked and texted every day over the next week. I prayed that Marcia wouldn't change her mind about the DNA test.

I made sure to lay it on thick, checking up on her each day and pretending that we were on the way to getting back together. She didn't seem suspicious.

Marcia called me on Friday night, saying she was in labor.

"Are you sure?"

"Yes, I'm sure. My water broke."

I texted Kenzie to tell her the news, then headed to the hospital. Marcia was already on the way there in an ambulance.

A text buzzed in from Kenzie a few minutes later. *Good luck. And I pray the baby is healthy, regardless of the outcome.*

Thank you.

I wanted to say more, but this was still a delicate situation for both of us.

I arrived at the hospital and was surprised to see Marcia's mom, though I shouldn't have been.

"Hi Karl," she said, then she looked around. "Is your mother coming too?"

I shook my head. "No Ma'am. She's not feeling well tonight, but she promised she would be here tomorrow."

Marcia's mother gave a look of disapproval before she nodded. "Okay. Well at least you're here."

She huffed away as if she was offended.

I felt like scum for lying on my mother. She wasn't aware of the plan Kenzie and I cooked up, but I would be sure to explain it to her later.

We entered the labor and delivery section of the hospital and Marcia was already wearing a hospital gown. She grabbed the railing and let out a guttural moan when we entered the room.

"Mom, it hurts so bad!" she wailed, and her mother rushed to her side.

I stood there awkwardly for a second, then jumped into action, rushing to her other side.

The doctor came in and informed us that since Marcia's contractions were coming in a rapid succession, there was a strong chance the baby would be born tonight.

They measured her to see how far she was dilated.

"Oh yes," the doctor said with a grin. "We are not too far away at all. Only a few more hours, Marcia."

Marcia was not happy to hear that it would be hours before the baby came.

Her contractions were severe and she almost crushed both me and her mother's hands, but thankfully, in another two hours, she was dilated enough to get the process started.

At some point, I switched out of my act and became sincerely concerned for Marcia and the baby.

I was all into it, talking to her and encouraging her, telling her she was almost there and that the baby was going to be fine.

Her mother seemed to appreciate my gestures.

At eleven-fifty-two, Tina was born at seven pounds and twenty-two inches.

Tina passed all the tests with flying colors.

She looked just like Marcia.

The strange thing was, although I helped Marcia through the birthing process, when Tina came out, I felt absolutely nothing. I was happy she was healthy and glad Marcia pulled through safely, but for the child, I felt no connection.

I hoped that wouldn't be a problem, especially if she was mine.

Chapter 27

The next morning, Marcia's family started coming in with balloons and flowers and looking at me like I was crazy because no one on my side had showed up.

Marcia's father arrived before everyone else because he worked an overnight shift nearby.

"Karl, didn't you say your mother was coming this morning?" Marcia's mother asked with a tired look on her face.

My heart fluttered. "Oh, yes ma'am. Let me go call her now."

I rushed into the hallway, kicking myself along the way. When I was safely out of earshot of all Marcia's relatives, I called my mother, explaining to her why she needed to come to the hospital as soon as possible.

"You did what, Karl?" was her shrill response.

"I know, Mom, I'm sorry. I just really wanted to know the truth."

"You know better than to be putting me into some mess."

I straightened up at her stern tone. "I know, Mom, I'm sorry. Can you please come?"

She sucked her teeth. "I guess so, Karl, since she might actually be my grandchild. I wish you would have told me Marcia was in labor. Now you have me looking bad to those people. You know me and Marcia's mother never got along as it was."

It was true. Marcia's mother always looked down on my mother for being a single mother and she had made a few comments when Marcia became pregnant before we got married, saying that she didn't want her daughter to end up like *some people*.

My mom caught the reference and they almost got into it, but she also wanted us to get married so the baby wouldn't be born out of wedlock.

My mom arrived with flowers, balloons, and a few baby toys an hour later. She gave me a cross look, then proceeded to be on her best behavior, holding the baby, *oohing* and *aweing*, and holding civil conversations with Marcia's family.

Despite the happy occasion, I could not wait to escape. I wanted nothing more than to see Kenzie. I hoped that things wouldn't change for the worse between us now that the baby was born.

Kenzie texted me asking how things were going, and I shared with her the details about Tina.

Congratulations, she said, but offered nothing more.

"Lord please," I prayed silently.

I stayed a few more hours at the hospital, then made an excuse about having to go home and change. I promised to be back and to bring Marcia anything she needed.

Of course, her mother disapproved of my decision, but I couldn't shake the internal tension I felt with the whole situation.

I did go home and shower, but instead of heading directly back to the hospital, I drove around aimlessly, contemplating what I was going to do if the baby was mine and Kenzie left me.

The DNA test could not be completed quickly enough.

Chapter 28

Marcia was home now, and I had stayed there a couple nights, using vacation time from my job to be there for her and help take care of Tina.

Her mom and my mom also showed up to help us.

On the third day, I told Marcia I was heading to the store, but I was really going to Kenzie's house. I hadn't seen her since the baby was born and I missed her like crazy.

It was strange how I still felt absolutely no connection to Tina, but my feelings for Kenzie had only intensified.

When she opened the door and saw me, I swore she was feeling the same.

"Hey," she said, letting me in.

"Hey."

We hugged.

She pulled back first and said, "How are things with the baby?"

I sighed. "Just waiting for the DNA results."

We had sent off for them before we left the hospital.

Kenzie's eyes grew glossy. "Karl, what are we going to do if she's yours?"

I swallowed. "I don't know, Kenzie. But I don't want to lose you."

"I don't want to lose you either," she confessed, "but I don't know if I can..." She didn't finish her sentence.

She didn't need to because I already knew what she was saying.

Although it would break my heart if we had to end our relationship, I wouldn't be able to say I blamed Kenzie. If the shoe was on the other foot and she had been pregnant with another man's baby before we met, would I have still married her?

"We can only pray for the best," I said.

"Right."

We stared at each other for a few moments, and my mind flashed through our whole relationship, from the first time we FaceTimed, to the day Kenzie got baptized and I was the one to do it, to our first kiss, to...

"Karl!" Kenzie croaked, then she reached up and swiped a tear from my cheek. "Don't cry. You're going to make me cry!"

She was already crying.

I wouldn't have realized I was shedding tears until she pointed it out to me.

"This is the craziest situation I have ever been in in my life," I declared.

"Same here," she said with a chuckle. "To have everything you ever wanted standing in front of you, only for there to be a chance that it's all stripped away."

I wanted to tell her that didn't have to be the case, that we could still work through it if the baby was mine, but I knew that would be empty words.

The truth was that eventually reality would hit.

Even if we started off strong, the baby would inevitably cause conflict between us. Not to mention Marcia and her ways.

"I'm still holding out hope," I said, my gaze never wavering from hers.

"Me too." She blinked back more tears, and before either of us knew it, I had grabbed her and swept her up into a kiss.

I could only pray it wouldn't be our last.

Chapter 29

I preached a heartfelt sermon for Youth Sunday as Pastor Blake had asked me to, but my heart wasn't fully in it. I loved the youth and wanted the best for them, but this situation with Marcia was causing me to lose sleep.

Every day I was checking the mailbox, only to see the results hadn't arrived yet. Me and Kenzie talked about it every day, though she still hadn't made her final decision about what she wanted to do if Tina was mine.

Marcia was over the moon with excitement. She adored Tina and was taking very good care of her. Tina was a beautiful baby girl and she barely cried, only if she was hungry, tired, or needed to be changed.

I took that as a blessing because although I was helping take care of her as much as I could, it hurt my heart that this little girl potentially had a father who either wouldn't be in her life or would only be there out of duty.

It drove me crazy that I didn't feel anything for her.

I took pictures of myself with Tina, as well as Tina by herself, and Marcia thought it was cute, but I really only did it so I could study the photos late into the night, trying to see a spark of resemblance between us.

Tina looked nothing like my baby pictures. Even my mother confirmed it when I told her what I had been doing.

"Karl, don't stress yourself," she had said. "If the baby is yours, I trust you will rise to the occasion and be the man I raised you to be. If not, you better count your blessings and never get yourself wrapped up in a situation like this again."

"I swear I won't," I said.

Mom had been a huge support through the whole process, despite the fact that she was initially upset with me when Tina was born.

She showered Tina with affection as well whenever she stopped by, and her and Marcia had a few pleasant conversations.

I couldn't help but to notice that Marcia's mother seemed to make it a point not to be there when me or my mother were there though. I didn't know what the woman's problem was. It wasn't like we had done anything to her or her daughter.

I was on my way home from church after Youth Sunday when I got a call from my mom.

"Hey," I said. "What are you up to?"

"Just got home from church," Mom said. Then she let out a breath before she said, "Karl, can you come by?"

Alarm bells rang through my mind. What was wrong with Mom? I was already making a U-turn and heading in her direction. "Are you okay?" I asked.

Her tone wavered. "I think so. I just need to tell you something."

My heart dropped.

I prayed it wasn't bad news.

My mom was getting up there in age. She hadn't had any health scares as of late, and aside from her car accident a while back, she seemed to be doing great.

Lord please, I prayed silently. I would not be able to breathe if something happened to my mother.

I arrived at her house in half the time it would have normally taken to get there.

I knocked on her door and bounced on the balls of my feet until she opened it.

When she did, I studied her, my eyes surveying her entire body for signs that something was wrong.

Aside from the fact that she was teary eyed, I saw nothing obvious.

"What is it, Mom?" I asked and followed her to the living room.

Unlike the last few times I had been here, Mom's house wasn't filled with the pleasant aromas of her cooking.

My nose burned with a fresh bout of emotion, but I held it back. Just because she wasn't cooking didn't mean anything.

Mom sat across from me on her loveseat, while I took the couch. There was a folded white sheet of paper next to her.

What was that? A diagnosis?

I braced myself for whatever she was about to tell me.

"What is it, Mom?" I said, barely breathing.

She sighed. "I finally did it, Karl."

"Did what?" My anxiety was killing me.

She picked up the paper and handed it to me.

My heart pounded as I opened it, reading it so fast I barely processed the words. When I saw what it was, I almost fainted from relief.

It was a divorce decree. "Oh, thank God," I said, then looked back at her.

Mom was crying silent tears. "I knew I had to do it. I thought it would be harder, and that the court clerk would shame me, and that your father... I didn't know why I made it more than what it was. Everything went smoothly. It should be finalized in a few months."

I stood to give her a hug. "I'm proud of you, Mom. You need to live your life and be happy. Find another man who deserves you."

Mom clung to me tightly. "Oh, I don't know about that, Karl. No man is going to want me. I'm all old and used up."

"Far from it! Ain't no momma of mine old and used up. You're only as old as you feel, and I swore the last time I visited your church, Deacon Charles was eyeing you."

Mom blushed. "He was not! You're just saying that." A look of hope flashed across her features.

"Mom, I'm serious. You are a beautiful woman, inside and out. Go through your healing process and allow yourself to be free. The Lord will take care of you just as He has been doing all this time. You will be fine."

Chapter 30

On Monday, I stopped by Drew's house after work to play videogames and catch up with the fellas.

"Any news yet?" Solomon asked after dapping me up when I entered the basement.

I dapped DeMarcus up first, then said, "Not yet. Hopefully soon."

"Dang, what's taking them so long?" Drew asked.

"How long did they say? Two weeks?" asked DeMarcus. "That's how long it took when I got mine."

All of our heads whipped toward him.

The words tumbled out of Solomon's mouth. "Your wife cheated too?"

DeMarcus shook his head. "No, it was me, remember? When I cheated, we had a scare, but thankfully, the baby wasn't mine."

"Oh." Solomon visibly relaxed, then he turned to me. "Well, I hope the same for you, man."

"Shoot, who are you telling? Me too!" I said.

We shared a laugh.

"What's Kenzie saying?" DeMarcus asked.

I shook my head. "She still hasn't made her decision."

Solomon stood. "Man... Let us pray."

We thought he was joking first, but when he held his hands out, we all stood in a circle holding hands, and Drew led the prayer. I felt every word in the pits of my soul.

I prayed that the Lord would hear it, along with all the prayers from me and Kenzie.

Marcia called me while I was on the way home, asking if I could come by for a couple of hours so she could take a nap, and to bring some more pampers.

I went to the store and picked up a few packs.

There was an older woman in the aisle with me, browsing different diaper brands as well. She reached to grab a box from the top shelf but couldn't get it because she was too short. I went and got it for her, placing it in her cart.

"Thank you, young man," she said.

"No problem, Ma'am."

She stared into my eyes as if looking through me.

It made me nervous. "Is everything okay?" I asked.

"You've had a cloud around you," she said.

"Huh?" I wrinkled my nose.

She stared at me further. "God said you've been going through a storm, but sunshine is near. Everything you went through was to teach you a lesson, but now that you've learned it, get ready for brighter days."

I didn't know how to respond to that so I thought it best to keep my mouth shut.

The woman continued. "You're reluctant to believe me, I know. Who am I but some old crazy woman buying diapers for a newborn?"

I was about to tell her I didn't think she was crazy when she spoke again.

"Check the mail, baby. Your answer came today."

The hairs on the back of my neck stood up.

Her eyes pierced mine for a few more moments before she turned and walked away.

Who was this woman?

At first, I did think she was kind of crazy, or one of those older people who always felt the need to prophesy to somebody, telling them the Lord told them something when they really made it up themselves. But she said my answer came today, and to check my mailbox! How could she possibly have known?

I exited the store and stopped at my house first, curious to see if the lady had really spoken a word from God.

My heart deflated when I saw that it was empty.

Dang, that older woman seemed so sure...

Oh well, I needed to get to Marcia's house.

When I got there, I took Tina and Marcia headed toward her room for a nap.

"Wait," I said, as she was turning her doorknob. It had just dawned on me that the results would be sent to both of our addresses. Perhaps Marcia had gotten hers today, which would confirm what the older woman had said.

"Yes?" she said, tensing up.

"Did you check your mail today?"

"Yes. The results haven't come yet, Karl." Her voice was cross, like she was tired of me asking her if she received the results. It was true that I asked her almost every day if she got hers, but she didn't have a real reason to be upset with me.

Still, I remained cordial. "Okay, thank you. Go ahead and take your nap."

She entered her room and I heard her snoring minutes later.

While she was asleep, I played with Tina a little, fed her, then changed her. Before rocking her to sleep, I stared into her eyes as if she would hold the answer to my question.

Of course, she didn't.

But now that Tina was asleep...

It was probably wrong to go snooping, but I couldn't help it. Marcia had shown herself to be a blatant liar. I wondered if she had received the letter but lied and said she didn't.

I crept over to her end table where she usually kept her mail and sifted through the envelopes.

Nope, it wasn't there.

"What are you doing?"

I jumped at the sound of Marcia's voice. She was standing in her doorway, rubbing her eyes.

I placed the envelopes back on the table, then picked up the remote. "Nothing, I was about to watch some TV."

She stared at me, then rolled her eyes. "Okay, Karl," she said, then went to the bathroom before going back to bed.

Another hour later, she emerged from her bedroom.

"Thanks for watching Tina," she said.

"No problem," I said, then I rose to leave. I faked a yawn. "See you later, Marcia. I gotta get some rest for tomorrow."

"No problem. Hey, could you take the kitchen trash out on your way out?"

"Sure." I went to the kitchen and changed the bags, but as I was closing the bag full of trash, my eyes caught an envelope with the DNA office's address on it.

Liar!

I carefully slipped the envelope out of the trash, but of course, it was empty.

I wasn't about to dig through the rest of the bag for the letter. Marcia had probably ripped it to shreds or something.

This made me furious, but I resolved to play it cool.

I would get my letter soon enough, and this whole situation would be over. If Marcia was hiding the fact that she got the letter, that could only mean one thing.

I exited her house without incident, heading home to take a quick shower before bed. Maybe my letter would come tomorrow.

A minute after I locked my front door, a knock sounded.

"Who is it?" I asked, then opened it when I heard my neighbor's voice on the other side.

It was Mr. Jones from two doors down.

"Hi Karl, I saw you walking up to your door from my window but I didn't get outside in time to catch you. I believe this is yours." He handed me an envelope.

It was from the DNA office!

"Wow, thank you!" I said in amazement. The lady at the store was right!

"No problem," he grumbled. "I sure hope the new postal worker doesn't keep mixing up our mail. Daggone millennials!"

I let out a chuckle as Mr. Jones continued grumbling as he made his way back home.

I wanted to rip that envelope open and get my answer right then and there, but my heart leapt with excitement as I thought of Kenzie.

She answered on the first ring. "Hello?"

"The results came!"

"What did they say?" Her tone matched my excitement.

"I don't know. I want us to see them together."

"Okay, come on over."

I raced back to my car and headed to Kenzie's apartment, knowing in my soul that the nightmare was finally over.

She was standing at the door waiting for me when I pulled up.

"Hey," she said, and we shared a hug.

I pulled back and handed her the envelope. "I want you to see it first."

She stared at me. "Okay..." Then she ripped it open, unfolding the letter that was inside.

As she read it, her eyes welled with tears. "Oh, Karl..." She looked at me, then covered her mouth, the waterworks breaking loose.

My heart dropped. That wasn't the reaction I expected. "What happened?"

I was so sure. The envelope was in Marcia's trash! The older lady said...

I took the paper from Kenzie and scanned the letter.

There was zero percent chance I was the father.

Kenzie's tears were happy tears.

"Thank God!" I sighed, then Kenzie grabbed me, clinging tightly around my neck.

I hugged her back with the same intensity.

"Okay, I can't breathe," she joked after a few moments.

I pulled back and we both swiped away tears.

She giggled, then wagged her finger at me. "You better not ever hold a secret from me again!"

I held my hand over my heart, feeling giddy as well. "Scouts honor."

She cocked her head to the side. "Boy, what did I tell you about that?"

Things got pretty passionate after that. There was a whole lot of hugging and kissing and caressing, to the point that I almost threw her over my shoulder and carried her to her bedroom, but the Lord spoke into my spirit and told me to calm down.

I obeyed.

"See you tomorrow, baby..." I said in a husky tone.

She snorted. "I ain't say I was taking you back!" Then she smirked, and I leaned down to kiss her again.

On my way home, Marcia sent me a text message. *What time are you coming tomorrow?*

I waited until I parked to write back. *I'm not.*

Seconds later, my phone rang. "Hello?" I answered in a cool tone.

"What do you mean, you're not coming tomorrow, Karl? You said you would help me get her ready for the appointment."

"There's no need for me to do anything else for you or your child, Marcia. She's not mine."

"What? What are you talking about? The results haven't come back yet!"

I let out a sarcastic chuckle. "You know, you really need to stop lying. It doesn't suit you. I saw the empty envelope in your kitchen trash, but you must have forgotten they were sending the results to my address too. I saw it with my own eyes. Please lose my number."

"Karl, wait!" Desperation filled her tone. "I can't raise this baby on my own. I... it was between you and another man. He's married."

"Just like I'm about to be," I said without missing a beat.

"What? I thought you and Kenzie..."

"I lied," I said, cutting her off. "Yes, it was wrong, but you lied first, Marcia, and you lied repeatedly. I knew there was another man involved. Make sure you give Bishop Wilkins and his wife my best."

Marcia gasped.

Suspicion confirmed. Bishop Wilkins from Holy Redemption church was Marcia's baby father, or at least I suspected as much until Marcia just admitted it through her reaction.

After Kenzie's former coworker Sherita told me how she found out about me and Kenzie's engagement, I did some investigating of my own.

The Bishop had posted one too many heart emoji's on Marcia's pictures to not raise red flags. He was one of several married men on her friend's list.

I enlisted the help of DeMarcus, Solomon, and Drew to get information from members of his church and apparently, there were whispers of Marcia going to his office for *counsel* almost every Sunday. Then when she started showing, the rest of the congregation had a field day, placing bets that the Bishop was indeed the father.

"There's no way you could know that!" Marcia sputtered.

"Save it," I said. "You need to repent, much less tell the Bishop about his new bundle of joy."

"Karl, please... I can't confront that man and his wife. The whole church will shun me!"

"Then maybe you will finally learn your lesson. I sure learned mine. Goodbye."

CLICK.

I hung up and blocked Marcia from my phone and all my social media accounts.

Chapter 31

I stood at the altar, holding hands and staring down into the eyes of the woman I loved. We had gone through the storm and the rain together, but the only thing holding us back from one another now were our vows and the veil that was covering Kenzie's face.

She was breathtakingly beautiful in her white princess gown, and I knew I was looking good too in my freshly tailored white tux with the golden cuff links.

Pastor Blake continued. "It is now time for these two dear souls to exchange their vows."

I swallowed. This was it.

"Karl, please take Kenzie's hand and place the ring on her finger, repeating after me."

I turned back and took the ring from Solomon, blinking away a tear as I turned back toward Kenzie.

Although my boys had played a silly game of *rock-paper-scissors* to see who would get to hand me the ring, I secretly hoped it would be Solomon. He was the one who went the hardest for me in trying to find out whether Bishop Wilkins could potentially be Marcia's baby father, and he was the one who initiated the prayer that night we received the DNA results.

Pastor Blake began. "I Karl, take you Kenzie, to be my lawfully wedded wife. To have and to hold, in sickness and health, for better or worse, for richer or poorer, forsaking all others, til death do us part. I solemnly vow this in Jesus' name."

I repeated, fighting not to get choked up, but Kenzie snorted when I got to the part where I said *forsaking all others.*

I burst out laughing too, and before we knew it, all of my groomsmen and her bridesmaids were in on the joke too.

Once the laughter died down, I finished my recitation and slid the ring on her finger.

She repeated the same vows back to me after taking my ring from her friend Kristi.

Pastor Blake smiled at us.

"Karl, do you promise to take Kenzie to be your lawfully wedded wife in front of God and all of the witnesses today?"

"I do," I said without hesitation.

He turned to Kenzie, asking her the same.

"I do," she echoed, smiling that beautiful smile once more.

"Then by the power invested with me, through our Lord and Savior Jesus Christ, I now pronounce you husband and wife. Karl, you may kiss your bride!"

I couldn't whip that veil back fast enough.

As Kenzie and I kissed, I felt warmth spread through me. I knew beyond the shadow of doubt that whatever trials we may have faced from this day forward, we would face them together and come out victorious.

"Alright now, that's enough! Save some for the honeymoon!" Pastor Blake joked.

Kenzie and I pulled back and laughed together, raising our enclosed fists in victory, then we jumped the broom that Kristi and Solomon placed in front of our feet.

It was a sunny and beautiful day outside. A warm breeze flowed through the park where we took our pictures, and I didn't have to hound the photographer to know they all came out perfect.

The reception was also awesome.

Kenzie and I danced the night away, surrounded by our family and friends.

At the end of the night, however, it was on and poppin'.

We headed straight to a hotel to *get to know each other more completely* before the official start of our honeymoon in Punta Cana. Our flight was scheduled for tomorrow morning.

Epilogue

Two years later...

Kenzie and I were still going strong.

Our marriage so far had its ups and downs, but thankfully the bad days were about silly things like me leaving the toilet seat up or her getting an attitude during her cycle.

Nothing serious.

Mom and Dad's divorce finalized shortly after me and Kenzie's wedding, and to Mom's utter surprise, Deacon Charles from her church actually did have a thing for her.

His wife had passed several years prior, and he wanted to make a move on my mom, but knew she was still married to my father.

When her divorce finalized, Mom gave a testimony about it during Sunday service. Deacon Charles waited a couple of weeks before he approached her, asking for her number.

They had been dating for six months when he popped the question, and a month later, they held a small ceremony in my mother's backyard.

After their nuptials, Mom urged me to build a stronger relationship with my father.

"Karl, I knew you held yourself back from him out of loyalty to me, but there's no need for that. I've finally moved on and I'm happy, but it would break my heart to know that I was the reason you didn't have a solid relationship with your father."

I followed her instructions and me and my father went out once a month for drinks and to talk about the game.

My brothers and sisters and I also hung out from time to time, and to my surprise, Kenzie actually grew closer to my sisters than I did.

Yet another reason to fall deeper in love with that woman.

Me and Kenzie's friendship circle was also solid as ever. With eight married couples between us, there was never a dull moment. From fish fries to game nights to couples' cruises, we were living our best lives.

My boys held me down through thick and thin, and I knew Kenzie would say the same about her girls without blinking an eye.

We heard through the grapevine that Marcia and Bishop Wilkins' affair got exposed. Apparently, his wife followed him one day, suspecting that he was cheating and saw him go into Marcia's house, only to emerge three hours later with his shirt wrinkled and the buttons of his pants lopsided. She confronted him, then played a recording of their conversation over the loudspeakers during the announcements at church.

Chaos ensued of course, and the Bishop was forced to step down, while his son, an upstanding man of God, took his place and fought to rebuild the church.

I could not thank the Lord enough that Marcia's lies were exposed and that I was not the father of her baby.

I had kept my promise to Kenzie and hadn't told a lie or held a secret since.

She often joked that I was *too honest* now.

I had recently been promoted to a supervisor position at my facility, which meant that it would be extremely rare for me to have forced overtime anymore.

Like I mentioned before, I loved my guys, but I would much rather spend every moment I could with my beautiful wife.

I headed to work Monday morning ready to bang out an eight-hour shift and then surprise Kenzie with a night out on the town.

I had already picked the perfect restaurant - a new seafood spot that had just opened downtown. Kenzie loved crab legs. I wasn't a fan of seafood, but thankfully, the restaurant also served chicken and steak, and that twelve-ounce New York Strip was calling my name.

My mouth watered just thinking about it.

On my lunch break, I prepared to text Kenzie to ask how her day was going and to tell her about my plans for our date.

Before I could reach her name in my contacts, a call came through from her.

"Hello, my lady," I answered with a smile in my voice.

Kenzie's voice was frantic, immediately causing me to stand at attention. "Karl! Come home, please, I need you."

"Wha...huh? I thought you were a work?"

"I left early. There's an emergency. Hurry, baby please!"

"Oh my God, okay, I'm leaving now." My mind began racing. "Hold on, let me tell my superior then I'm on my way."

"Okay..." Her voice wavered as she spoke. "Please hurry."

My body grew hot and cold as I ran to my boss to tell him what was going on.

"Go ahead, Karl. We got you. Please let us know if you need anything."

I barely heard what he said as I practically ran out of the building, hopped in my car and hightailed it home.

Kenzie's car was outside.

I clicked my key fob to lock my doors then ran up to the front door of the home we had just purchased last year.

The door was unlocked, so I bounded inside, sweat pouring down my forehead. "Baby? Baby, where are you?"

Kenzie emerged from our downstairs bathroom, wearing a black lace teddy with a mesh robe that hit the tops of her thighs and left nothing to the imagination.

She strutted toward me, a seductive smirk etched across her lips and held out a white test stick.

"Welcome home, Daddy," she said, then waited as I looked at the results.

My jaw dropped and my eyes bulged in their sockets. "You're pregnant?"

She nodded, then my heart skipped a beat as she leapt into my arms.

The End

Dear Reader,

I'm so glad you chose to read the finale to this series. Karl's story took me on an emotional rollercoaster, and I'm sure you felt the same.

Although this is the end of Kenzie and Karl's story, I have another story cooking in the kitchen. Harmonie's journey is a rocky road, filled with secrets, pain, and triumphs. Check her out in Pray for Me: Struggles of a Broken Heart.

See you soon!

Neesh Santiago

Before you go...

If you enjoyed *Better Late Than Never 2*, I would greatly appreciate it if you could leave a **rating** or **review**. Not sure what to say? Simply comment on your favorite character or overall thoughts of the story. It only takes a couple of seconds, and it would help boost the visibility of this book so that others may enjoy it as much as you (hopefully) did. I would love to hear from you!

PS: To connect with Neesh Santiago, join her email list at neeshsantiago.com/subscribe.

Follow Neesh on social media!
Facebook: Neesh Santiago
Instagram: @neeshsantiago
Twitter: @NeeshSantiago

TikTok: @neeshsantiago
YouTube: Neesh Santiago
YouTube: Uncovering Christ
Website: neeshsantiago.com

Discussion Questions

Dear Reader,

Karl's story dealt with some controversial issues. My alpha team described it as an emotional rollercoaster that had their hearts racing and kept them on the edge of their seats.

If you felt the same and are part of a book club, here are some potential questions to get the conversation going:

1) Do you think Karl took too long to tell Kenzie about Marcia's pregnancy?

2) If you were Kenzie, how would you have responded? Would you have seen the baby as an issue or went on with the marriage?

3) What did you think of Karl's mother's story? As a follow-up, do you think the church sometimes puts too much pressure on women to be wives and mothers?

4) Comment on Karl's friends versus Kenzie's friends. Who would you want on your team?

5) Do you think Christians are able to remarry after divorce in God's eyes?

6) Do you think there is redemption for a spouse who cheats? In other words, is the saying, *once a cheater, always a cheater*, true?

7) What did you think of Marcia's character? Do you think Karl should have handled her differently?

8) How do you think the story would have ended if Karl was Tina's father?

9) What was the most shocking or surprising part of this story for you?

10) What was your favorite part of this story? Would you recommend it to others?

Hopefully these questions will be helpful in sparking a great conversation!

Want another story by Neesh Santiago? Check out Harmonie's story in <u>Pray for Me: Struggles of a Broken Heart</u>.

Neesh Santiago's Books

Better Late Than Never
Better Late Than Never 2
Pray For Me

Neesh Santiago's Journals

A Page In My Rhyme Book
A Page In My Song Book
A Page In My Poetry Book
A Page In My Bible Study Journal
A Page In My Spiritual Goals Journal

Neesh Santiago's Album
(available on all streaming platforms!)

Forever Changed

Neesh Santiago's Merch

T-shirts, hoodies, and more!

About the Author

Neesh Santiago is an author, rapper, spoken word artist, Bible teacher, and faith-based entrepreneur. She was born and raised in Springfield, Massachusetts.

Neesh has been rapping and writing since her early teens and has participated in numerous open mics, competitions, and more, including winning the first-place prize at her Alma Mater, American International College's talent show in 2008.

Her debut album, Forever Changed, was released in 2022 with much more to come. Her debut novel series, "Better Late Than Never" is the first, but certainly not the last story that will demonstrate Neesh's mission of "**Penning Truth To Power**" through Christian fiction and nonfiction books.

Printed in Great Britain
by Amazon